JOYCE CAROL OATES   YIYUN LI   JOHN CURRIN

WALTER ROBINSON   PADGETT POWELL   AN-MY LÊ

HOFFMAN   SHEILA CALLAGHAN   AIMEE BENDER

CHRISTENSEN   ZHANG HUAN   DANIEL WALLACE

JANE SMILEY   NICKY BEER   SIMON RICH

GIDEON BOK   RUTH REICHL   SWOON   SONYA CLARK

ESMERALDA SANTIAGO   LAURIE HOGIN   NIKKI S. LEE

ALEXIS ROCKMAN   T.C. BOYLE   ELIZABETH ALEXANDER

PAUL MULDOON   ROZ CHAST   ELISSA SCHAPPELL

MARINA ABRAMOVIĆ   HENRY ALFORD   HEIDI JULAVITS

MUEENUDDIN   CHRISTINE SCHUTT   JULIE HEFFERNAN

TAVARES STRACHAN   FERNE JACOBS   BHARATI MUKHERJEE

KREIDER   JULIA ALVAREZ   NATALIE EVE GARRETT

THE
ARTISTS'
AND
WRITERS'
COOKBOOK

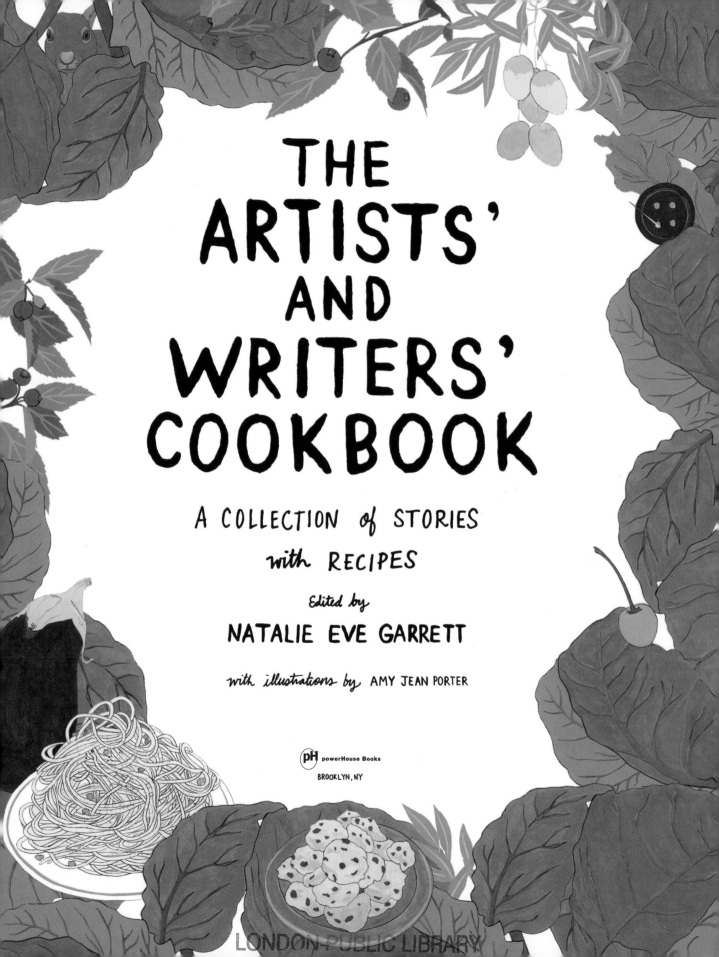

THE ARTISTS' AND WRITERS' COOKBOOK

A COLLECTION of STORIES with RECIPES

Edited by

NATALIE EVE GARRETT

with illustrations by AMY JEAN PORTER

powerHouse Books
BROOKLYN, NY

For T,

Sf, and Lio

&

for artists and writers
everywhere,
with love.

SNACKS

SWEETS

INTRODUCTION

The Artists' and Writers' Cookbook is a secret portal into the kitchens of 76 contemporary artists and writers.

It's also a collection of personal, food-related stories with recipes. The dishes range from Joyce Carol Oates' "Recipe in Defiance of Grief" to James Franco's PB&J with a pickle on the side, encompassing a diverse group of celebrated artists and writers.

The idea for this book solidified when I stumbled upon a cookbook that's older than I am: *The* [original] *Artists' & Writers' Cookbook,* published in 1961, which included recipes from the likes of Marcel Duchamp, Man Ray, Marianne Moore, and Harper Lee. It's a deceptively plain-looking book; as soon as I got hold of my own copy, I couldn't put it down. I knew right away that it would be a thrill to create a modern version.

In the book from '61, Duchamp, for example, shares his recipe for steak tartare: "Let me begin by saying, ma chere, that Steak Tartare...is in no way related to tartar sauce. The steak to which I refer originated with the Cossacks in Siberia, and it can be prepared on horseback, at a swift gallop, if conditions make this a necessity." Cooking on horseback with Duchamp! As I read, I felt like I was sharing food and swapping stories with him and the other artists and writers. It seemed so intimate and unexpected, and—okay, let's be honest—a little bit crazy.

But the more I read, the more the connection between art, writing, and cooking made sense: Ideally all three are about making something new. They all require some measure of vision, revision, faith, and magic, not to mention a high tolerance for disaster. All three also engage the senses, surprise and sustain us, and can be evocative. And, at their best, they can even be transformative. Plus, almost everyone has one good food story and recipe to share.

For me, as an artist and writer who loves to cook, making something new often involves making a big mess, which is part of why I prefer to paint, write, and cook in private. But maybe leaving a trail of mistakes is also part of what connects art, writing, and cooking; mistakes remind us of our humanity, and can even lead us towards something great.

When I invited artists and writers to share recipes for this collection, I honed in on "Americans," while also choosing to include American expats and people born elsewhere in the world currently living in the U.S., even if only temporarily. Most of all, it was important to me to present artists and writers with varied perspectives and dishes to share. I asked contributors to tell me about the last memorable dish they made or the food they eat while writing or drawing or falling in love. I asked for old hand-me-down recipes, accidental recipes, dream-recipes, unusual interpretations of the idea of a "recipe," or simply trusted standbys. The only requirement was that each recipe have a story.

The result: a collection of essays that range from funny to wrenching to restorative, coupled with memory-laden recipes that are a pleasure to read and recreate. Many are delicious too, although the book encompasses the imaginary, the charmingly bizarre-gross, and the almost-disastrous.

While each contributor interpreted my invitation in their own way, the pieces explore common themes of childhood, transition, homecoming, authenticity, love, and loss. Artists and writers recall food that offers both comfort and challenges—food that honors tradition and dares to forge something new.

In this book, Anthony Doerr lures us out into the wild to find huckleberries and happiness. Neil Gaiman makes a perfectly eerie cheese omelet while Ed Ruscha associates his cactus omelet with "a time of doom." Yiyun Li eats rations in Beijing while Edwidge Danticat prepares a soup to celebrate freedom. Nelson DeMille reminisces about a meal he ate 40 years ago when serving in Vietnam; Kamrooz Aram recalls childhood "picnics" in his basement in Tehran during air raids. Sanford Biggers updates a soul food classic—"something tasty to lessen the bitter taste of consistent, systematic oppression." Paul Muldoon and Aimee Bender conjure food-related apocalyptic visions. Marina Abramović shares a dish best consumed on top of a volcano, Elissa Schappell dreams of playing Serge Gainsbourg records to snails, and Padgett Powell tastes a dish that reverses time and space. Daniel Wallace woos with an eggplant sandwich. Francesca Lia Block tells us how to fall in love.

The real joy comes from discovering this portal into the kitchens and personal lives of beloved artists and writers. Let's jump in.

Natalie Eve Garrett

BREAKFAST

ANTHONY DOERR
HUCKLEBERRY MUFFINS
A.K.A. HAPPINESS

Rent a cabin in Idaho's West-Central Mountains. Preferably in July. August will work.

Park your car or drop your bike beside a logging road and plunge into the underbrush. Head uphill. Chances are the stuff scratching up your legs will be huckleberry bushes. Be sure to bring along a plastic milk jug with the top sawed off. A half-gallon is best.

Sometimes out-of-towners can't see the berries at first, so give yourself time: they're smaller than pencil erasers, they look like little violet blueberries, and they like to hide under the leaves. Bringing kids will help.

Huckleberries are exasperating to cultivate, and I've heard they're good for you, but that's not why you're doing this. You're doing this because frozen huckleberries are never as good as fresh ones; because they stain your fingertips so purple they're almost black, because bears love them, because birds love them— half the bird shit in these mountains in July is purple. You're picking wild huckleberries because they taste like long starlit nights and cold dewy mornings and hot afternoons when the sun brings out the sap in the pines. You're doing this because you only get so many summers in your life, so why not be out beneath the sky, amongst the trees, stuffing your mouth with something sweet?

I like to average two in the jug for every one in my mouth, but you'll work out your own ratio. Plip, plip, plip, the huckleberries fall into your jug, the soothing sound of incremental work. You're running a marathon, composing a symphony, one berry at a time. After a half hour, some small and utterly reliable transformation will take place: the mind quiets, the body enters the oldest kind of memory. This, after all, is what we are, we humans: foragers. We like to tell ourselves that our lives are richer than those of our Stone Age grandparents, but is the equation so simple? The men and women who walked these forests 9,000 years ago could read stars, turn spear points, track prey, mend clothes, predict storms, and start fires. They were fit, lived on a hugely varied diet, and never stood in queues nor hunched over iPads. Were their lives more violent than ours? Maybe. Maybe not.

Imagine if every plant, bird, and rock around you meant something: shelter, medicine, a memory, a landmark. Listen to the chipmunks around you, and the birds, and the deer. There is great strength in knowing where your food comes from.

Stay until you're tired, until the light changes, until the mosquitoes come out, until your kids want to go home, until everyone's lips are stained purple. Pedal your berries home and set them in the fridge. Pour wine. Grill something. Friends will tell jokes like, "I went to the zoo the other day; there was only one dog in it; it was a shitzu," and maybe it's the sunset or the wine or the berries, but everything will seem deeply funny. Laugh.

That's called happiness.

And so is this: in the morning, while everyone else is still in bed, rinse a couple handfuls of huckleberries. You'll never get all the stems out; stems are part of it. If a little refrigerated spider is hiding in there, so be it.

Mix the ingredients and pop the muffin tin in the oven. After 10 minutes, the kitchen will smell like cinnamon, butter, and benevolence. Repeat this recipe often enough and it will start to smell like nostalgia. After 15 minutes, kids will wander in, dragging blankets. After 20 minutes, the adults will come hunting coffee. Take out the muffins.

Don't let them cool for long; you want the insides to steam. You want hot huckleberries to explode between your teeth. You want to watch everyone close their eyes when they eat. Out there, beyond the windows, trout rise in the lakes; pileated woodpeckers hammer dead trees; a last wolverine dozes beneath a slab of granite. A pair of bear cubs are sitting with their mother in a berry patch, harvesting drops of sugar from the cradle of the season. You'll never be connected to this world like your ancestors were, but for a moment, with the purple stain of summer in your mouth, you can try.

Huckleberry Muffins

1 ½ cup flour
¾ cup sugar
2 teaspoons baking powder
½ teaspoon salt
1 egg

⅓ cup vegetable oil
⅓ cup milk
huckleberries (at least two big fistfuls)
cinnamon
butter
brown sugar

Combine the flour, sugar, salt, and baking powder. Add the egg, oil, and milk. Drop in the huckleberries, mix, and pour the batter into the cups of a greased muffin tin. Top with a crumble of cinnamon, butter, and brown sugar (to taste), and bake at 400 degrees.

ANTHONY DOERR's most recent book is *All the Light We Cannot See,* which won the 2015 Pulitzer Prize for fiction and was a finalist for the National Book Award. His short stories have appeared in *Best American Short Stories, The O. Henry Prize Stories, New American Stories,* and *The Scribner Anthology of Contemporary Fiction.* Doerr lives in Boise, Idaho with his wife and sons.

LEANNE SHAPTON
IN THE NIGHT KITCHEN

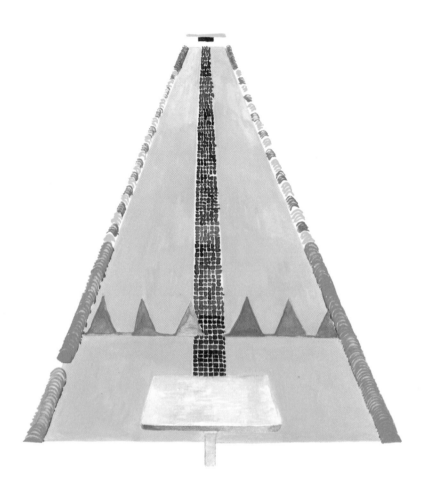

In February 1987, my alarm clock would go off at 4:25 every morning for swim practice. My routine was this: From the bed, I reach for the two damp swimsuits drying on the bedroom doorknob, take off my pajamas, pull the suits up halfway. Under the covers, I pull on track pants, three T-shirts, a sweatshirt and two pairs of socks, which had been piled at the foot of my bed the night before. Once dressed, I switch on my bedside lamp, wincing.

The hour between four and five a.m. is a dreadful hour, especially in the dead of Canadian winter. Knowing I have to get into a chilly pool and endure two hours of unrelenting muscle pain makes it worse. But I love the

quiet, the bluish-blackness out my bedroom window, less menacing than midnight dark. I like riding next to my mother through our suburban streets, bundled into a team parka, listening to the sound of the car tires squeak over the packed snow.

These days when I wake between four and five a.m, I read, I ruminate, or, I bake. The kitchen is a changed place in the wee hours, its clicks and hummings are louder, pots and pans make a deafening clatter when I pull them out of the cupboard. But I am relaxed, my sense of smell is sharper. As I measure and weigh, I am patient. I've always turned to flour and butter when I can't sleep.

On swim practice mornings, I'd sometimes bake too, or rather, microwave: a mucky invention I called "Muffin-In-A-Mug." Quaker instant bran muffin mix, a splash of milk, stirred, nuked for 2 minutes and then eaten with a spoon. It would be half bready, half raw, but delicious, sweet, and warm. I'd bring it along in the car if we were running late, spooning the stuff into my mouth with mittens on, as I watched icy streetscapes swoosh past.

I had a ritual, while I waited for my muffin-in-a-mug to cook: I put my batter-filled mug in the oven and set the time to 1:11:00, the time I wanted to swim the short-course 100 meter breaststroke in 1987. Then I cover my eyes with a hand, finger on the start panel, imagining my starting block, and the pool: a vast table of smooth water, still and clear. I see the dirty grout between the small white tiles on the bottom. The lane ropes pulled taut along the surface. I can hear teammates in the stands and families in the gallery. A long sharp whistle calls us to the blocks. The quiet is sudden. My hands reach to touch the front of the sandpapery block, between my toes.

I push start on the microwave. Breathe, dive. In the kitchen, in my track pants, there are eight or nine strokes the first length, a double handed touch, and silence underwater at the turn. I hear a faucet upstairs turn on, then off. In my mind I am ahead, no one in my periphery. My legs start to tire. I lay a hand on the countertop at 50 meters, legs and chest hurting. Halfway down the pool on my final length I hear sharp beeping and open my eyes, the microwave is flashing 00:00:00. Too slow by about five seconds. I cook the muffin for 45 more.

Muffin-In-A-Mug

¾ cup Quaker instant bran muffin mix (available in Canada)
¼ cup milk

Combine in mug. Microwave for 1:56:00.

LEANNE SHAPTON is an artist, author, and publisher based in New York City. She is a regular contributor to *The New York Times* and the author of *Was She Pretty?, Important Artifacts...,* and *Swimming Studies,* winner of the 2012 National Book Critic's Circle Award for autobiography. Most recently, she coedited the bestselling book *Women in Clothes* with Sheila Heti and Heidi Julavits.

MAILE MELOY
ANTI-INFLAMMATORY MUFFINS

My mother stayed with a friend in Seattle earlier this year, and came home on the friend's "anti-inflammatory" diet. It was mostly a social gesture, as my mother has no health problems but lots of enthusiasm. And it made her cook more often and eat less sugar: admirable goals for anyone. She showed me the cookbook, which had a blurb on the front that said, "The diet that has taken Vashon Island by storm!" My husband, who thinks all diets are eating disorders, said, "Vashon Island! It might get to Tacoma next—or even Spokane!"

One of the rules of the diet is no grains at breakfast, which posed a barrier to my joining the island cult. In the morning, you're supposed to eat half protein and half fruits or vegetables. But breakfast, to me, is grains, and I need it to be very simple: a bowl of cereal and a cup of tea. The great benefit of working in the morning is the closeness to sleep and the subconscious. If I had to stop, chop vegetables, crack eggs, and apply heat, my brain would become too crowded and distracted to get anything done. I told my mother so.

"You can eat muffins for breakfast!" she said, triumphant.

"With no sugar or grains?"

"You make them in advance," she said, "with almond meal and sweet potato. I have two for breakfast, with fruit." She produced a muffin, and it was surprisingly good. It seemed generous of the no-sugar diet to allow fruit and sweet potatoes. Milk in your tea is okay, too—or half and half in your coffee. Even very dark chocolate is fine. It's a friendly diet that allows for pleasure, and I thought I could at least follow it for breakfast.

I made a batch of muffins when I got home, and my husband took half of them to work. Mid-afternoon, his colleagues said, "You got any more of those muffins?" But they were gone. I am not a food hoarder, and I believe that baked goods are for sharing. But the almond meal had been hard to find and startlingly expensive, and those muffins were supposed to be my week's breakfast. I said, "You can't take all of them to work."

He said, "Uh-oh. Are you going to get all inflamed now?"

Here is the recipe, with thanks to the Abascal Way cookbook. It's been modified by my mother's friend's memory as she wrote it up in an email, my mother's commentary on that email, and my own experimentation.

I can tell if a batch is really good or not, because the good ones still vanish to the office, one or two at a time. When they're less successful, I have muffins all week. If you share living space and want quick, reliable morning sustenance, you might want to make them less tempting, so I've included ways to do that.

Anti-Inflammatory Muffins

2 cups almond meal
2 teaspoons baking powder
½ teaspoon salt
4 eggs
1 cup cooked mashed yam/sweet potato
1 mashed banana
½ cup unsweetened applesauce (optional)
¼ cup olive oil
fresh fruit, dried fruit, nuts (optional)

Bake a sweet potato or two—the day before, if you can. My mother throws two in the oven whenever she's baking something else. I use the soft orange ones that are sometimes called yams, and you can pierce the skin with a fork or cut them into a few round pieces. Once they're baked (about 45 minutes at 400), the skin peels off easily. Put the flesh in the refrigerator to be muffin-ready. If you have to bake, peel, cool, and mash while you're prepping the muffins, you might get impatient and skip the sweet potato in favor of extra bananas, but that makes the muffins so dry and bland that you won't want to eat them.

Preheat the oven to 350.

Combine almond meal, baking powder, and salt. I do this in the big measuring cup, to save dishes. (Almond meal is available at most grocery stores with the other Bob's Red Mill flours. It's $11 for a smallish bag that makes two batches, but just think about what you'd pay at a coffee shop for a single inflammatory muffin.)

Beat eggs with a whisk to get some air into them.

Add cooked mashed sweet potato, mashed banana, and unsweetened applesauce to the eggs. Lazy mashing with a fork is fine. This step is very adaptable: you just want 2 cups of mush. White sweet potatoes are drier, so using those, or skipping the applesauce, will give the muffins the texture of baked sawdust and stave off thieves. Pumpkin or squash will work, too, but who wants to bake a pumpkin? Canned pumpkin will tempt you to use the whole can to avoid waste, in which case the muffins will ooze out of the paper wrapper and be impossible to transport.

Add olive oil. (This is a step I often forget and have to do at the last minute.)

Combine the dry ingredients with the wet, and mix well with the whisk or a spatula.

Add any fruit, nuts, or spices that you like. I've been using 1 teaspoon ginger, the zest and juice of a small lemon, and fresh blueberries. I tried dried, unsweetened Bing cherries and toasted pine nuts once, and got to keep all the muffins for myself, but I was sick of them by the second day.

Line a 12-muffin tin with paper liners and spoon the batter in. You could grease the tin if you had no liners, but these muffins really stick. Sometimes I have extra batter when I go overboard with the yams or banana, and I use a lined ramekin for the extra.

Bake 25–30 minutes at 350, or until the tops are golden brown. Let cool, and refrigerate the ones you're not going to eat soon, ideally in the back of the refrigerator where they won't be found.

In the morning, split the muffins and warm them up in the toaster (if they're firm) or the microwave (if they're gooey) and add a little butter or yogurt on top. Eat two, with some fruit if you want, and go to work.

MAILE MELOY is the author of the novels *Liars and Saints* and *A Family Daughter*, the story collections *Half in Love* and *Both Ways Is the Only Way I Want It*, and the Apothecary trilogy for young readers. She has received *The Paris Review*'s Aga Khan Prize, the PEN/Malamud Award, the Rosenthal Foundation Award from the American Academy of Arts and Letters, and a Guggenheim Fellowship. Born in Helena, Montana, she now lives in Los Angeles.

JOYCE CAROL OATES
RECIPE IN DEFIANCE OF GRIEF

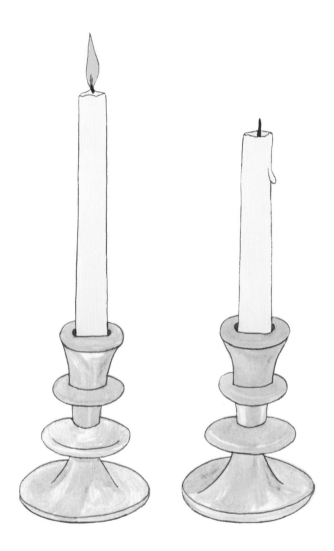

Something simple like scrambled eggs with onions and smoked salmon and a particular sort of sourdough bread, and he might've had a glass of wine, possibly two glasses of wine, and there'd certainly have been a salad, mostly red-leaf lettuce, though with some of those little red cherry tomatoes he grew in his garden; and thin-sliced cucumbers, and thin-sliced red peppers; for it's a household custom for him to make a simple meal when you've been traveling, and to put a small vase of flowers on your desk for you to discover when you return. And it comes as a slow revelation to you—(you who are dazed with travel, both at the time and now years later recalling that time as across an abyss of such depth and vertigo you dare not glance into it)—that yes, this is the last meal he will prepare for the two of you, the last meal he will prepare on such an occasion, or on any occasion, on this wintry evening in February 2008, as it is the last time you will set the table for two and light the dining room candles in the glass-walled house; and so you are thinking that possibly you can't prepare the simple meal that had been one of your customs, for it's too soon, and you aren't ready; you aren't strong enough; a recipe in defiance of grief is one of those gestures thrilling in poetry but unrealizable in life because in life we are often not strong enough to execute the wishes we have set for ourselves though these are laudable wishes. So thinking *Maybe another evening, maybe this year, or next. Or maybe not ever. And to whom will it matter?—almost no one. Just one.*

Scrambled Eggs, Onions & Smoked Salmon

4 eggs, scrambled
chopped onion
minimal butter
small pieces smoked salmon

In frying pan melt butter and cook onions.

Add pieces of salmon.

Stir in scrambled eggs.

JOYCE CAROL OATES is the author of a number of novels as well as plays, volumes of poetry, short story collections, innumerable essays and book reviews, and longer nonfiction works. She has written some of the most enduring fiction of our time, including the national bestsellers *We Were the Mulvaneys* and *Blonde*, and the *New York Times* bestsellers *The Falls, The Gravedigger's Daughter,* and *The Accursed*. Her most recent book is the memoir, *The Lost Landscape: A Writer's Coming of Age.* She lives in Princeton, New Jersey, where she is Distinguished Professor of Humanities at Princeton University.

YIYUN LI
HOPE IN A THIN SHELL

When I think of food, I think of queues. I was a child of rationing, and a big part of my education about the world and the people who inhabit it came from queuing for food. This was Beijing in the 1970s, and most of the things on our table—rice, flour, oil, pork, fish, eggs, milk, sugar, sesame paste, tofu—were rationed.

What was not rationed were the marvels a child could find in the world. Every Sunday I went shopping for food with my father. There was always more than one queue, and my father would install me in the longest one before joining a shorter one himself. The queues moved at the speed of a worm. It took courage and faith for a child of four or five to stand in line alone with people several times their size threatening to cut in. To secure my place I learned the trick, much to the frustration of whoever was in front of me, of pressing myself tightly to their backside. And then there was the fear that would never go away: what if I reached the front and my father didn't show up? What if I were abandoned in that line forever?

But he did always come back in time, so I learned to enjoy the wonders in the shop. It had an overhead transit system with motorized lines zigzagging around. The shop assistants would attach the payments to metal clips, the money would travel to the cashier and later the change would travel back. There was an apparatus fixed to the giant jar of cooking oil, and when each person handed a bottle to the assistant, he would only need to raise a lever to release the right amount of oil through the funnel into the bottle. On the counter were huge chunks of pork that looked inviting, though the slice the assistant cut for us always had more fat than lean meat—but don't ever think of complaining, because the moment you opened your mouth he would withdraw the meat, and others would ask for it. Rationing didn't mean you could always get your share.

Among the marvels, there were glimpses of grim reality. A man walked from line to line, saying he had lost his family's ration book: had anyone picked it up? But no one would meet his pleading eyes. Another time, a crowd gathered to watch two women calling each other nasty names. One was foxier than the other, and stood accused of using her charms to get a better slice of pork. From time to time the shop assistants, reigning from the other side of the counter, would stop to have a long chat about a movie, just so they could keep everyone waiting. One day the line spilled outside the shop, and I watched a bus pull in. The conductor leaned out of the window, looking at an old man running to catch the bus. The moment the old man reached the door, panting, the conductor hit the button and banged the door shut, waving goodbye with a wide smile.

If you were a child of the rationing system, sooner or later you learned that it wasn't just food that was rationed. So was hope, dignity, comfort, love. When my mother heard that I had cried for the old man, she dismissed my tears as shameful, saying my heart was too soft.

But even that soft-hearted child could find the goddess of fortune smiling on her. Standing in the queue one Sunday, I noticed a basin of eggs on the counter. It can't have been the first time it had happened, as I already knew that one lucky customer would get that basin of eggs, sold off cheap and—best of all—not recorded in the ration book.

We waited for the shop assistant to point her magic finger. It picked out my father and she said the eggs would be ours if we wanted. I trailed home a step behind my father, watching more than a dozen eggs, yolks and whites, floating in a clear plastic bag. It was a warm day and we didn't have a refrigerator, so my father cooked them right away, and I found myself tucking into a plate of scrambled eggs.

If you were that child of the rationing system, you'd have never seen such luxury. You would grow up and always feel hope when you see a full plate of scrambled eggs. That feeling is still there 30 years later, but it comes with another shadow. The day you were lucky enough to get a basin of eggs, you also watched a long line of strangers eyeing you with jealousy, even hatred. You were not who you were, but what you were rationed to be.

Scrambled Eggs

12 eggs
canola oil
salt

Whisk a dozen eggs with a pair of chopsticks, add a spoonful of warm water, a pinch of salt and whisk well.

In an iron wok, heat a small (minimum) amount of canola oil until very hot.

Pour in the egg mix, stir until the eggs are set.

YIYUN LI is the author of the story collection *A Thousand Years of Good Prayers*, which won the Frank O'Connor International Short Story Award, PEN/Hemingway Award, and Guardian First Book Award; the novel *The Vagrants*; the story collection *Gold Boy, Emerald Girl;* and most recently, the novel *Kinder Than Solitude*. She has received numerous awards, including the Whiting Award, a Lannan Foundation Fellowship, and a MacArthur Foundation Fellowship. She was selected by *Granta* as one of the 21 Best Young American Novelists under 35, and was named by *The New Yorker* as one of the top 20 writers under 40.

JOHN CURRIN AND RACHEL FEINSTEIN
DIFFERENT PALETTES

The first meal I made for John was scrambled eggs with garlic and onions, and he gobbled up every last bite. Back then he was so in love with me, he didn't dare say anything. Little did I know that he despises garlic and onions—it wasn't until years later that he told me that the dish actually made him sick. Now, after 21 years together, he knows me well enough to tell me whether or not he likes the food.

John and I grew up with wildly different childhoods and palettes. He lived in Santa Cruz until he was ten, when his family moved to Stamford, Connecticut. At home, they cooked standard American cuisine; his favorite dish was called the "Hawaiian"—a sweet chicken with pineapple and cashew nuts. They never went out to eat.

I was raised in Miami, and we ate out often. In fact, my parents would plan faraway trips just around the food. Before I turned 16, we had traveled to China, Russia, Greece, France, England, and Italy, and we ate well everywhere—except on one memorable occasion, on a trip to London. My dad's company sent us all out for a day trip to the Tate Gallery. We walked in the door and immediately my parents decided they were too hungry to see any art, so we went to a fancy sit-down restaurant in the gallery. When we didn't recognize anything on the oddly medieval-themed menu, we all ordered pigeon pot pie, which turned out to be a whole bird cooked in aspic—basically a savory brown jello encasing a pigeon. It was horrible (and it also cost about 500 pounds!). But mostly I have a lot of delicious food memories from all over the world.

I think it's partly because I was exposed to so many different types of cuisines and spices that I became an adventurous eater. John did not. Instead, John has many food aversions: He hates anything with cumin in it, as well as most Middle Eastern spices. He can't stand garlic and onions unless they are cooked to death. But—perhaps because he was raised in Santa Cruz—he's always enjoyed Mexican food, despite the heavy use of garlic, onions, and even cumin.

This recipe for scrambled eggs with tortillas was inspired by something my friend, the great painter Jacqueline Humphries, made for me and my family when we visited her and her husband Tony Oursler a couple of years ago. It pairs well with homemade guacamole. And, most importantly, John gobbles up every last bite, with pleasure.

Mexican Eggs

3–4 corn tortillas, cut into long, thin strips
8 large organic eggs
¾ cup shredded cheddar cheese
1 medium tomato or 1 cup salsa
4–5 scallions, diced
3 tablespoons cilantro
2 tablespoons vegetable oil

Heat oil in frying pan on medium heat. Beat eggs in a medium sized bowl. Add tortilla strips to heated oil. Add pinch of salt and sauté until slightly browned. Add diced scallions and cook for 30 seconds. Add eggs to pan. Continually stir mixture until eggs are not runny but not super firm. Turn off heat and add cheese to top. Remove from pan and top with cilantro, sour cream, and tomatoes and/or salsa. Serves 4–5.

JOHN CURRIN's ambitious paintings seduce, repel, surprise, and puzzle. With inspirations as diverse as Old Master portraits, pin-ups, pornography, and B-movies, Currin paints ideational yet challengingly perverse images of women, from lusty nymphs and dour matrons to more ethereal feminine prototypes. Consistent throughout his oeuvre is his search for the point at which the beautiful and the grotesque are held in perfect balance. Currin (b. 1962, Boulder, Colorado) received a BFA from Carnegie Mellon University and an MFA from Yale University. His work is represented in museum collections worldwide, including The Museum of Modern Art, New York; Tate Collection, London; and Centre Georges Pompidou, Paris.

RACHEL FEINSTEIN is known for her rococo-inspired, monumental sculptures that are imposing in scale yet often delicate in their use of materials. Alluding to fairy tale and myth, her works are littered with art historical references, whether an homage to Arte Povera or a nod to classical notions of beauty. Feinstein (born 1971, Defiance, Arizona) studied at Columbia University and Skowhegan School of Painting and Sculpture. Her work has been the subject of numerous exhibitions, including "Something About Mary," Metropolitan Opera House, New York; "Rachel Feinstein: The Snow Queen," Lever House, New York; and "The Little Black Dress," SCAD Museum of Art, Savannah, Georgia.

ED RUSCHA

ED RUSCHA'S CACTUS OMELETTE: A DISH FOR MORNING, NOON, OR NIGHT

To me, the idea of eating cactus suggests saving yourself at the last minute in the desert at a time of doom.

One day, shopping in a Mexican market, I came across a jar of nopalitos that shouted out some kind of possibility. Akin to the sliminess of okra, with a subtle flavor that's vaguely like pickles, the cactus seemed to ask to be mixed with eggs, although mixing these ingredients has probably been going on for ten centuries south of the border.

When fellow artist and Californian Doug Aitken asked me to contribute something to his "Station to Station" project, food-on-a-train came to mind and I had visions of rolling through the desert in a Super Chief dining car. Cactus omelettes on a choo-choo train seemed to be more than compatible.

Ed Ruscha's Cactus Omelette

2 eggs from any farm
2 tablespoons small curd cottage
   cheese
2 tablespoons diced celery
3 tablespoons diced cactus
   (nopalitos, usually sold in jars
   in international food section
   of grocery)
1 tablespoon sweet butter
salt, pepper

Utensils: omelette pan or similar
   type with rounded bottom, mixing
   bowl, wire whisk or fork

Break eggs into bowl. Slightly under-mix with whisk or fork. Heat butter in pan until it bubbles and begins to turn brown. Add eggs and let them sit there until the bottom begins to harden. At this point, lift the edges ever so slightly, so that the runny top layer can slip under on all sides. As soon as this sets, but while the top is still moist, add the salt, pepper and cottage cheese in a line down the center, as you will be folding the omelette in half. Sprinkle the celery on top of the cottage cheese, followed by the nopalitos. Fold the empty side over so that it produces a half-circle. Let the omelette set for about one minute over low fire. Roll omelette out of the pan and onto plate.

For people who like shaggy dog stories, add little bits of the green cactus on the top of the omelette to make sad or funny faces.

ED RUSCHA's photography, drawing, painting, and artist's books record the shifting emblems of American life in the last half century. His deadpan representations of Hollywood logos, stylized gas stations, and archetypal landscapes distill the imagery of popular culture into a language of cinematic and typographical codes that are as accessible as they are profound. Born in Omaha, Nebraska, in 1937, Ruscha studied painting, photography, and graphic design at the Chouinard Art Institute (now CalArts). His work is collected by museums worldwide. He is represented by Gagosian Gallery.

NEIL GAIMAN
CORALINE'S CHEESE OMELETTE

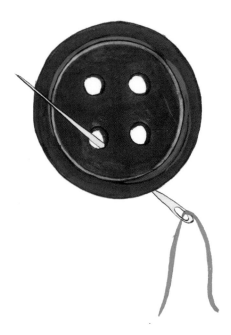

Her other mother smiled gently. With one hand she cracked the eggs into a bowl, with the other she whisked them and whirled them. Then she dropped a pat of butter into a frying pan, where it hissed and fizzled and spun as she sliced thin slices of cheese. She poured the melted butter and the cheese into the egg mixture, and whisked it some more.

"Now, I think you're being silly, dear," said the other mother. "I love you. I will always love you. Nobody sensible believes in ghosts anyway. That's because they're all such liars. Smell the lovely breakfast I'm making for you." She poured the yellow mixture into the pan. "Cheese omelette. Your favourite."

Coraline's mouth watered. "You like games," she said. "That's what I've been told."

The other mother's black eyes flashed. "Everybody likes games," was all she said.

"Yes," said Coraline. She climbed down from the counter and sat at the kitchen table.

The bacon was sizzling and spitting under the grill. It smelled wonderful.

"Wouldn't you be happier if you won me, fair and square?" asked Coraline.

"Possibly," said the other mother. She had a show of unconcernedness, but her fingers twitched and drummed and she licked her lips with her scarlet tongue. "What exactly are you offering?"

"Me," said Coraline, and she gripped her knees under the table, to stop them from shaking. "If I lose I'll stay here with you forever and I'll let you love me. I'll be a most dutiful daughter. I'll eat your food, and play Happy Families. And I'll let you sew your buttons into my eyes."

Her other mother stared at her, black buttons unblinking. "That sounds very fine," she said. "And if you do not lose?"

"Then you let me go. You let everyone go—my real

father and mother, the dead children, everyone you've trapped here."

The other mother took the bacon from under the grill and put it on a plate. Then she slipped the cheese omelette from the pan on to the plate, flipping it as she did so, letting it fold itself into a perfect omelette shape.

She placed the breakfast plate in front of Coraline, along with a glass of freshly squeezed orange juice and a mug of frothy hot chocolate.

"Yes," she said. "I think I like this game."

Cheese Omelette

2 eggs
butter
cheese
1 tablespoon milk
a pinch of salt

Beat together eggs, milk, and a pinch of salt.

Melt a large pat of butter in the frying pan, coat the pan with it, then pour it into the egg mixture and beat it in.

Pour the mixture into the pan.

Sprinkle grated cheese onto the omelette.

Push the eggs away from the edges of the pan, letting anything liquid cook. Don't let the bottom of it brown. Fold it in the pan or do the elegant thing where you slip it half onto the plate then let the top half come down on the bottom half. Garnish with fresh parsley or don't, depending on the finickiness of whoever you are feeding and whether or not they are scared of parsley.

NEIL GAIMAN has written highly acclaimed books for children and adults and is the first author to have won both the Carnegie and Newbery Medals for the same work—*The Graveyard Book.* Many of his books, including *Coraline* and *Stardust*, have been made into films. Neil's more recent titles include the *New York Times* bestselling short story collection, *Trigger Warning,* and his enchantingly reimagined fairy tale, *The Sleeper and the Spindle* (with illustrations by Chris Riddell). Born in England, Neil now lives in the United States with his wife, the musician and author, Amanda Palmer.

WALTER ROBINSON
DESIRE

As a 30-something artist living in a tenement apartment on the Lower East Side, I ran at full throttle. I showed my paintings of kissing couples at Metro Pictures and at galleries in the East Village, compiled art news items for *Art in America* magazine, and was unpaid art editor at the *East Village Eye*. I was a member of Collaborative Projects, a multidisciplinary artist collective that organized exhibitions, ran an art space, and a movie theater, and produced a weekly cable TV show—among other things—serving as the group's president for a year.

And that was just what happened during the day.

When I did stop to eat, I would cook myself real food: burgers, meat loaf, pot roast, paella, chili. Basically, I ate whatever I wanted. I denied myself nothing. My art was all about desire, and as a 1960s love child, appetites and passions played a big part in my life.

After I got married, my wife, a former Chanel model who taught herself art restoration, gradually edged me out of the kitchen. She insists on what she calls a "clean" menu: fish, chicken, vegetables, and grains, with no exotic sauces or spices. The food is simple but delicious, and easy to cook—another virtue, from her point of view.

A virtuous diet suits me. Inevitably with old age, my metabolism has slowed down. I rarely eat desserts anymore, and bread, pasta, and rice are off limits. Even fruits are restricted, since they've been masterfully cultivated to be as sweet as any candy confection. Part of my new regimen is a sensible breakfast. That is to say: oatmeal. As it turns out, with a few judicious additions, even the humble rolled oat can become sumptuous.

I still paint the objects of desire, whether six-packs, pin-ups, or pancakes. Though I've never painted a bowl of oatmeal, but—perhaps I should.

Oatmeal Assemblage

½ cup oatmeal
1 cup water
dried cranberries
walnuts
apple pieces
blueberries
salt (optional)
maple syrup (optional)
low-fat cottage cheese (optional)

Take a little more than ½ cup "old fashioned" oatmeal and dump it into the saucepan. Fill your measuring cup with water to a little less than 1 cup, top it off with a bit of milk (it makes the oatmeal slightly richer), and add to the pan. Toss in a handful of dried cranberries.

Bring to a boil, stirring regularly with a wooden spurtle, a tool that actually makes the cereal better.

While the oatmeal cooks, peel half an apple and chop, you can eat a few pieces. And then chop some walnuts, not too many. The oatmeal won't take long to cook, it shouldn't be too dry.

Cover the oatmeal while you make your coffee.

Dish out the oatmeal into two bowls. It helps if they're nice, and not too big.

Sprinkle the apple and walnuts on top, and add some blueberries, too. For my oatmeal, add in a heaping tablespoon of low-fat cottage cheese, and it's ready to go. For my wife's, you should have salted the oatmeal when you put it in the bowl, and at the end add a touch of maple syrup. Try to eat it slowly, since it has to last you till lunch. Unlike a hobbit, you don't get a "second breakfast."

WALTER ROBINSON is a painter, art critic, and the founding editor of *Artnet Magazine* (1996–2012). The first museum survey of his work went on view in the fall of 2014 at the University Galleries at Illinois State University in Normal, Illinois, and opens at Jeffrey Deitch in the fall of 2016. He lives and works in New York.

SOUPS
&
SALADS

PADGETT POWELL
THE LUNACY OF GUMBO

About 35 years ago, 1980-ish, I was sitting one night in a kitchen in Scott, Louisiana, at a fake redwood picnic table on a fake redwood bench after a day of driving a van hauling musicians to and fro Barry Ancelet's Festival de Musique Acadienne et Créole and we had been drinking beer all day and had moved to Jamesons and it was maybe about 11 p.m., we'd passed Dan Jenkins's Stage 5 Fuck Dinner I would guess about six or seven, when Barry Ancelet, the dean of all things Cajun and a person of some quiet authority, said, "Let's have a gumbo!" and as I gathered he meant food I thought he'd lost his mind. He strode to the stove and cooked something and then from a chest freezer beside the stove got out some bricks of something frozen and as I continued to ply the whiskey and think he'd lost it he put the bricks of something in the pot with the other something and a neutron wave hit me, some gaseous sublimation of greenness and grease, that

arrested the march into oblivion completely. It reversed time and space to somewhere before Stage 5 Fuck Dinner, and it said I was going to eat something—all I had to do was find out what it was and get it out of that pot. And I had found—owing to this Cajun dean's lunacy, his deciding that falling-down drunk we would eat—one of my foods.

A man, unless he is a Frenchman, has only a couple of foods that command his attention. That he will read about, track down, travel for, presume to criticize others for liking poor executions of, etc. And that he will learn to make. We all have these, often to egregious effect, but sometimes not. I found out what gumbo is and have made it for 35 years. I can make it better than any commercial instance of it I have had except at Cochon in New Orleans by that chef whose name eludes because he did not answer my message when I wanted to profile him. I hope he is still alive because many of the people I have wanted to profile and haven't have died on me: in alphabetical order Bob Burns, original drummer for Lynyrd Skynrd, ran car into tree; Allen Collins, original guitarist with Lynyrd Skynyrd, complications from paralysis from running car into I know not what; Blackie Collins, knife designer, cf. Gerber LST, ran motorcycle into what I do not know; M.C. Davis, largest land conservator in the southeast United States, ran into Stage 4 lung cancer. I am not going any deeper into the alphabet and am not wanting to profile anyone at this point. I've killed enough as it is.

I made gumbo once to entertain at Peter Patout's house on Bourbon Street, and Slim, his houseman, who at first refused to have any of the gumbo, did finally assent to have some and said, eating his second bowl, "I'm shocked, you being from Florida and all." Another time at Peter's I put tomato in a seafood gumbo against Peter's counsel and ruined it. Gumbo is not a foolproof food. Care and very careful carelessness must be taken.

A Gumbo

bones and vegetable scraps for
  making stock
meat
(Andouille) sausage
roux
celery
peppers
onions
okra
tomatoes
parsley

I am going to say here some things that might accelerate you into grasping gumbo. Do some reading: look at *The Joy* of course, then read Paul Prudhomme as your real primer. Look at his pictures of roux making. See the one where the roux looks like Hershey's syrup. That is what you want. One is supposed to use a light roux with a dark meat, but I like to snort at this. There are not many dark meats anyway. Coon is a dark meat, but not many people are going to be making coon gumbo (they should). Withal, make the roux dark. Take time making it dark—not fast.

You may take 30 minutes or more toasting the roux. Do not feel that your life is wasting away, just wonder as you sweat over this stuff, constantly stirring it, what, say, Putin is doing at this very moment, if he has his shirt off on a horse and is cool. What became of Yeltsin?

The vegetables that go into stopping the roux will be rendered invisible. Only those added later will be present— okra, typically, but not in every gumbo, and green-onion tops, sometimes tomatoes that you want to see and feel. Both the invisible and the visible vegetables can be off-list. The on-list is celery, peppers, and onions, annoyingly insistently called The Trinity. I have used celeriac, leeks, weird peppers, eggplant, heavy parsley. I'd use a beet but the purple scares me a bit. Fresh peas would disappear very nicely in stopping a roux. Find what you have and have at it.

Use rich stock; make it yourself from every bone and vegetable scrap in the house. For seafood stock get big heads and backbones. Since you will have spent a fortune on the seafood your fish man will give you all the head and carcass you want.

Brown your meats in the oil you will use to cook the roux. Typically you want two meats (in seafood gumbo, several, though see below when I say goodbye). One meat can be thought of as an "accent" meat; it is commonly a cured meat or otherwise exotic compared to the main meat, and you use less of it. Sausage (the Cajuns call for andouille sausage but they do not mean true andouille, though if you can get actual andouille you should) is the most common accent meat. Squirrel is a good accent meat. Squirrel can

be the main meat. A squirrel gumbo can be insanely good. A squirrel tastes as good as the animal is athletic and smart. If they were not as athletic and smart as they are, they would not require extermination for the problems they cause, such as penetrating the attic and making alterations to the electrical scheme that are not up to code. But athletic and smart they are, and uncertified as electricians etc., so sometimes you find yourself with a supply of them for accent meat, or main meat, in gumbo. God had this Life Path more or less in mind for them, insofar as He is All-Seeing, but I do not think Darwin had the path in mind.

I was stumbling along on my Life Path one night when I went into a second-story bar in Matagorda Texas. Most likely this was before 1980, so it predates my experience with Barry Ancelet's undoing Dan Jenkins and the natural order of the universe. It was a Thursday night and Thursday night this bar offered free food. The free food was in a pot. It looked like Coca-cola. If you dug around in the coke with a ladle you brought up whole half crabs, without legs. White heavy crab chunks in shell. The liquor looking like coke did not taste like coke. It tasted good. Extremely good, and it infused the crab meat that you sucked out of the recesses of the shells from those plastic-y compartments separating

→

crab muscles. I suppose they are chitinous dividers. This crab was so good that you hollowed out the shells completely, then got more of the false-coke liquor. This was the best free food I have ever had in a bar. It would be the best food I have ever paid for in a bar had I paid for it. It was gumbo but I did not know that. The word did not cross the threshold until Barry Ancelet said it. But this nonetheless was it.

Okay, you are set. If you read a little and work at it, you and your Path will be changed and you will have proper gumbo. The chef at Cochon is Donald Links. I do not want to profile or kill him. I will certify his gumbo if you want to start there.

PADGETT POWELL has published six novels—*Edisto, A Woman Named Drown, Edisto Revisited, Mrs. Hollingsworth's Men, The Interrogative Mood, You & I,* and three story collections—*Typical, Aliens of Affection,* and *Cries For Help, Various.* His awards include a Whiting Writer's Award, the Paris Review John Train Humor Prize, the Prix de Rome, and the James Tait Black Memorial Prize in fiction. He teaches at MFA@FLA.

AN-MY LÊ
BÀ MÌNH'S PHỞ

We had just finished celebrating the New Year and gone to sleep when we were awoken by wild shouts, loud explosions, gun fires, and flares. The Communists had infiltrated Saigon and a small platoon was taking position in the recess of the entrance to our apartment building. They fought there until they were overrun at dawn.

I was born in Saigon and spent my early childhood there and in Huê, Vietnam. While I was too young to have been shaken by the fear, chaos, and helplessness of a daily life of war, I of course could not forget the Tết Offensive, and I still remember being dropped off at school early one morning, only to find the school gates demolished and still smoldering from a mortar attack.

My brothers and I would take this all in stride. Instead, we focused on the elaborate gatherings my maternal grandmother—whom we affectionately called Bà Mình, or grandmother ours—would throw for our extended family. For her, any occasion was an opportunity for an elaborate feast: exams, graduations, mid-autumn lunar festival, Tết, Christmas. She directed her army of cooks, suppliers, and volunteers with precision, and the culminating event never disappointed.

Within a few months of the Tết Offensive, my mother received a scholarship to return to France to work on her Ph.D. in English literature. My father could not leave Vietnam but they decided together that my mother should take the opportunity to advance her career and allow us children to live in more safe, normal circumstances for a few years. My brothers and I could hardly believe it; it seemed like something out of a fairy tale.

$\longrightarrow$

We arrived in Paris the summer of '68, not long after the momentous student uprising, and moved into Bà Mình's fifth floor walk-up apartment. She had come there a couple of years before us and had managed to secure a two-bedroom apartment in a maze-like and incredibly drafty housing complex for low-income Catholics in the 14th arrondissement.

My memories of that first autumn in Paris are dominated by games of tag and dramatic play in the courtyard of the public girls' school I was enrolled in. Wearing coveralls with our names hand embroidered on them, the girls and I chased each other around the chestnut trees, laughing and stomping on piles of brittle leaves. I also remember struggling: with spelling as the teacher intoned passages from Proust's *Remembrance of Things Past* for the weekly dictée and with memorizing one La Fontaine fable after another.

For the most part, though, I felt like any other French schoolgirl—until I came home from school. My mom would still be at the library doing her research, but Bà Mình would be there, enveloped in clouds of smoke, a cigarette dangling from her mouth, listening to Trịnh Công Sơn, the Bob Dylan of Vietnam, commandeering the apartment's kitchen and living room for her culinary experimentations. Looking up at me with a huge smile—she had lacquered black teeth, and wore her hair in the northern traditional style, slicked and twisted in a black velvet wrap which was then spun and pinned around her head—she'd beckon me to come try whatever she was working on. Then we would eat and critique the dish together.

At the time, there were a few high priced and mediocre Chinese restaurants in Paris. There was also one Vietnamese restaurant, located in the basement of a family grocery store that everyone in my family suspected was an informal gathering place for the Vietnamese communists of Paris. The dining room was painted hospital green and could only be accessed by a very steep, precarious wooden ladder. It opened on Tuesdays and Thursdays for lunch and served only one delicious dish, a northern Vietnamese style congee with tripe and blood sausage.

Within this bleak culinary landscape, Bà Mình resorted to taste and memory to conjure a complete repertory of Vietnamese home-cooked dishes. I quickly became her commis, taste tester, and sous-chef. Up and down the five flights of stairs and through the drafty passageways of the housing complex, I was often sent to look for "Chinese" parsley or cilantro at the various grocers and outdoor markets. *Ciboulette chinoise,* Chinese chive or scallion was relatively easier to find and fortunately the Communist grocery store had an endless supply of fish sauce. Until Asian ingredients were more readily imported, Bà Mình deftly played the game of substitution. And although we yearned for the real thing, we were always grateful to sit down to dinner and try one of her preparations.

These days, I can easily find a fragrant phở accompanied by the most elaborate platter of herbs such as spearmint, cilantro, Thai basil, and saw tooth coriander whether I am in Vancouver, London, Paris, New York, Los Angeles, or Sydney. But I still make Bà Mình's phở for my children on weekends when they are begging for it and we have run out of Asian ingredients. When I do, I think fondly of my time in Paris, and of course of Grandmother Ours, who recently passed away at the age of 102 while living in California.

Phở for 4

2–3 pints homemade chicken stock
1 onion with the last layer of skin on
1 2-inch piece of ginger
1 stick cinnamon
3 star anise
2 chicken breasts
a few tablespoons of fish sauce
salt (to taste)
5 black peppercorns
1 lime (or lemon) cut in small
   wedges
¼ cup of scallions or chives,
   finely cut
4 larger nests of dried egg
   fettuccini
4 large soup bowls

Put the onion and ginger under the broiler for about 5–7 minutes until they are charred. Turn them over and char the other side.

Toast the star anise, peppercorns, and cinnamon stick in a large stockpot at medium heat until fragrant and as toasted as possible without being burnt. Transfer chicken broth to stockpot with the toasted spices. Add the onion and ginger when they are ready and bring broth to a simmer. Add salt and fish sauce to broth to taste.

Poach the chicken breast for 15–20 min in the chicken broth until barely cooked through. Remove the chicken breast and let it cool, then shred it and reserve. Skim the scum from the surface of the broth every so often while the chicken is cooking.

Boil another large pan of water to cook the fettuccini. Add salt as if you were cooking pasta. Add the fettuccini and cook until very al dente. Drain the fettuccini in a colander and quickly run cold water through it to stop the cooking. Drain well.

Prepare the bowls by placing a very large handful of cooked fettuccini into each bowl. Spread the shredded chicken over the pasta and scatter the chives on top.

Check the broth. If it looks and tastes too concentrated, then dilute with some water—you will need about 3 pints of broth for 4 large bowls. Adjust to taste with salt/fish sauce if necessary. Once the broth is simmering, ladle it over the noodles and serve with a wedge of lime and sriracha if you have it.

AN-MY LÊ is a Vietnamese-American photographer whose work has explored the military conflicts that have framed the last half-century of American history: the war in Vietnam and the wars in Iraq and Afghanistan. Her latest project, *Events Ashore,* (Aperture, 2014) takes on the always polarizing and mythologizing representations of American military force. Her photographs have been widely exhibited and collected. She is a professor of Photography at Bard College and a 2012 recipient of the MacArthur Fellowship.

GREGORY CREWDSON
THE GREGORY CREWDSON SALAD

The Gregory Crewdson Salad is for the serious culinary aesthete only. No salad may bear the name The Gregory Crewdson Salad unless these instructions are followed in an exacting manner, following all rules and guidelines, with no deviation. No liberties may be taken, no ingredients swapped or altered, no room for subjective interpretation.

The construction of this salad is not just a meal, it is a challenge, a discipline, an experience, an adventure.

Before even thinking of making this salad, you must bear in mind the following imperative: All ingredients must be purchased in Massachusetts, at Guido's Marketplace, the Great Barrington branch. Period.

The Gregory Crewdson Salad

Equinox Farm mesclun mix (from loose bin, fill a plastic produce bag approximately half way)

shitake mushrooms from Ghent, NY (from loose bin, fill a plastic produce bag approximately one third)

1 black/green avocado (supple to the touch, not mushy)

1 medium-sized Vidalia onion

1 container small red tomatoes on the vine

1 ample handful of cashews (from Bin 189, roasted without salt)

1 container Oliva Lactinato Kale & Walnut Pesto

1 container Nuovo Ricotta & Parmagiano Tortellini

Peel the onion, cut in half, and slice lengthwise. Place the onion in a cast-iron skillet with olive oil over medium heat. Season. Cook the onions slowly, allow to caramelize.

Meanwhile, boil the tortellini to al dente texture. Drain. Add two tablespoons pesto. Toss gently. Set in refrigerator to cool.

Place mesclun in a large white porcelain bowl.

Put chilled tortellini atop mesclun in the center.

Chop avocado into small cubes. Place on top of tortellini.
Halve each tomato, add on top of avocado.

Over very low heat in a stainless skillet, toast cashews lightly. Add them on top of the tomatoes.

Place caramelized onions atop the cashews.

Snip stems from mushrooms, place in a cast iron skillet, season with salt and pepper and fresh thyme. Cook over low heat until crispy in 1 tablespoon butter and 1 tablespoon olive oil. The mushrooms are served in a separate, smaller, white bowl, on the side.

DO NOT TOSS SALAD AND DO NOT ADD ANY ADDITIONAL DRESSING.

Serve using two wooden spoons.

The Gregory Crewdson Salad is typically served with medium-well flame-grilled salmon, and a Red Bordeaux or Pinot Noir.

GREGORY CREWDSON is a photographer best known for his surreal, elaborately staged portraits of American homes and neighborhoods. His work has been included in many public collections, most notably the Museum of Modern Art, the Metropolitan Museum of Art, the Whitney Museum of American Art, the Brooklyn Museum, the Los Angeles County Museum, and the San Francisco Museum of Modern Art. He is Director of Graduate Studies in Photography at the Yale University School of Art and is represented by Gagosian Gallery.

EDWIDGE DANTICAT
SOUP JOUMOU

Our ancestors had been forced to abandon babies, parents, with both feet nearly in the grave. They had spent days under the sweltering sun, which was made all the more searing by rays bouncing off the boiling sea. Some had walked off the ships in the middle of the night, seduced by freedom and the phosphorescence of the evening sea. They had sunk into the water whispering, shouting *Ayibobo* or *Praise God.* When they landed, many had dropped themselves on the sand, rolling around until a grainy layer of gray covered them. Some picked up hard bitter sea grapes that had been scattered by the tide and quickly bit into them. Others gathered seashells and placed them between their teeth, as though they were jewelers evaluating gold. The world was still spinning as it had on the boat. They kept their backs to the sea, which it seemed to them had become one with the sky. No matter where they were on the new land however, they kept their eyes peeled for white faces. They kept their eyes peeled to the past but also the

future. They dreamed of shelter, food. They dreamed what they left behind, but they also imagined us, who lay ahead. They envisioned us into existence. They loved us. It is their love that brought us here. It is their love that keeps us here. We are the fruit of their struggles. And though it would not come for centuries, they imagined this day when we would gather at different points across different lands and the guns pressed against our temples would be gone, and the chains on our arms and legs would be shattered, and our muffled screams would become a roar, and we would raise our hands under whatever sky we found ourselves, and we will call both the names we know and do not know as we celebrate our freedom. And we would enjoy the fruits of the lands, sunset-tinged carrots and squash and grass green celery, the flesh and bones of bulls. And we would add our own touches to that meal, whatever the new harvest would produce, but we would always eat this meal, drink this soup, to celebrate our freedom, to erase a painful past, the ache of hunger in their bellies. We drink this soup on the first of the year, as a sign of our independence, as a celebration of a new beginning when it is said that whatever you do on that day will be replicated for the rest of the year. So if we eat the fruits of the land, during the first day of the year, the day we celebrate our freedom from oppression and slavery, hopefully we will always have plenty to eat, from our own sweat, from our own blood, and this painful journey across the seas will be a memory that inspires us to live, for our ancestors, for our children, and for ourselves.

Most Haitians eat soup joumou on the first of the year, on the anniversary of Haitian Independence Day. On that day, almost every Haitian family who can afford to will cook up a bowl of pumpkin soup. Soup joumou is also served in some households and in many Haitian restaurants on Sundays.

My recipe is not a master chef's, it is a very basic one. Everyone makes soup joumou differently; I make a vegetable-heavy vegan version.

Soup Joumou

1 pumpkin between 2–3 pounds, peeled and cut into small pieces
1 pound cabbage, sliced and chopped
4 carrots, peeled and sliced
3 stalks celery, sliced and chopped
1 large onion, cut into small pieces (if you prefer, you can cut it across, ribbon-like.)
5 potatoes, peeled and cubed
2 turnips, peeled and cubed (optional)
1 lime cut in half and squeezed for as much juice as you can get from it
¼ pound macaroni (In Haiti we call it vemisèl, but I have used different kinds of vegan pasta, including bow shaped. Some folks use spaghetti, whatever kind of pasta you can find is fine, but the pasta should not overwhelm the soup, so if you are using spaghetti for example, make sure it is broken into small pieces.)
3 garlic cloves, crushed or cut into small pieces
1 sprig thyme
1 sprig parsley
2 teaspoons salt
2 teaspoons ground pepper
1 Scotch bonnet pepper

Use a stock pot, if possible. Bring water to a boil, add pumpkin so that it is completely covered by water. Cook for approximately 30 minutes.

Once the pumpkin is cooked, purée it and add the purée back in the pot. Add more water if necessary for the consistency you desire.

Add the hard vegetables now: onion, celery, carrots, potatoes, turnip cubes and simmer for about 20 minutes or until cooked. Add cabbage, pasta and let it simmer until cooked. Add thyme, parsley, garlic, salt, and pepper until you are satisfied with the taste.

Add lime and stir in.

Add the Scotch bonnet at the last minute.

It is always an adventure in Haitian families to see who ends up with the Scotch bonnet at the dinner table. That is usually the person reaching for the water at 90 miles per hour. If you want just the flavor and not the heat, make sure you take out the now wilted Scotch bonnet before you serve the soup.

Turn off the heat and allow soup to sit in covered pot until ready to serve, with Haitian bread when possible. If Haitian bread is not available, a baguette or a similar type of bread will do.

EDWIDGE DANTICAT is the author of several works of fiction: *Breath, Eyes, Memory, Krik? Krak!, The Farming of Bones, The Dew Breaker,* and *Claire of the Sea Light;* numerous works of nonfiction: *Brother, I'm Dying (a memoir), After the Dance: A Walk Through Carnival in Jacmel,* and *Create Dangerously: The Immigrant Artist at Work;* as well as several picture books and novels for Young Adults. Danticat received the 2011 Harold Washington Literary Award in Chicago and was the recipient of a MacArthur Foundation Genius Grant in 2009. Her work has appeared in *The New Yorker* and in many anthologies.

ALICE HOFFMAN
MY GRANDMOTHER'S RECIPE FOR LIFE

Run away from men on horseback. Don't breathe. Don't cry out. Be silent and wait till they ride on. Then follow the path through the woods. Make sure there are potatoes in your suitcase. Ice can be melted from the river. Add berries to make tea. Add fresh mint. Drink deeply. Water will never taste like this again.

Share everything with your sister and brother, even if you go hungry. There's strength in numbers. Family is everything. One day your sister will save you from a trap made for wolves. Your brother will give you his boots on a snowy night.

Steal if you must. But only from a farmer's field, or from a shop where onions are piled in a basket. Never take anything from other people. They may need it more than you. They may be the border guard, the ticket salesman, the woman who will give you a map and a loaf of bread.

On a ship across the ocean, eat lemons. Keep lemons in your pockets, think of sunlight, think of another life, eat the rind, the seeds. For seasickness, tell yourself a story that takes place in a field of grass.

When you reach your destination you will see more

food than you knew existed. Noodles, bread with sesame seeds, roasted chickens, cakes with raisins and plums. These stocked store windows will make you happy to be alive, but also sad, because you can't afford anything. At least not yet. Get a job, make a salary, take in relatives, cook in a single pot, remember you can make anything taste better by adding an onion.

Don't forget potatoes. They got you through the forest, through the sea voyage, through the tent on the dock. Now they can be used to make a soup that is surprisingly delicious. Call it whatever you like. Call it the Recipe for Life. Don't forget to write it down for your daughter. You never know who will need it next.

Potato Soup

3 roasted garlic cloves, minced/ mashed
1 medium onion, chopped
2 leeks, chopped
3 large russet potatoes, peeled and chopped

½ cup butter
3 tablespoons olive oil
½ cup dry white wine, if you have it
4 cups water (or chicken stock)
salt and pepper to taste
chives

Sauté garlic, onions, and leeks with butter and oil on medium heat until translucent. Add the potatoes and sauté for 7 minutes. Add water or stock and wine, then salt and pepper. Purée if you wish. Hope for the best.

ALICE HOFFMAN is the author of nearly 30 bestselling novels including *Practical Magic,* which was adapted into a film starring Sandra Bullock and Nicole Kidman; the Oprah Bookclub Choice *Here on Earth;* and most recently *The Dovekeepers, The Museum of Extraordinary Things,* and *The Marriage of Opposites,* a novel about the life of Rachel Pissarro, the mother of Camille Pissarro, the father of Impressionism. Alice Hoffman also writes for teens and children and is the author of *Aquamarine, Green Angel,* and *Nightbird.* Born in New York, Alice Hoffman attended the Stanford University writing program, and currently lives in Boston.

SHEILA CALLAGHAN
BUTTERNUT BLUNDER

One Thanksgiving years ago, I was meeting my future husband's extended family for the first time. His mother and her people are from Cyprus, and his father and his people are from Greece. At the time they all lived in Toledo, Ohio. When I say "all" I mean a gaggle of relatives who fled their countries to escape Turkish oppression. While I am neither Greek nor much of a cook, I knew if I wanted to be an acceptable Greek wife to my future husband's family I needed to learn how to make at least one delicious dish that could feed 15 hungry Mediterraneans. So, I tasked myself to find a flavorful, idiot-proof, large-batch item in keeping with the brisk Midwestern autumn. I settled on a deceptively simple butternut squash soup recipe that uses Herbes de Provence as the forward flavor. I did a test run in my tiny Brooklyn kitchen. Easy and delicious.

I memorized the recipe on the plane so I could seem competent in the kitchen. After we dropped our bags off at my fiancé's childhood home, we set out to the local Kroger's. I found all my ingredients with one notable exception: Herbes de Provence. We tried three different markets. Nothing. I panicked. That herb mix is the very essence of this soup, the thing that makes it elegant and imposing. And, I had promised the soup to his family. I had to make the soup.

So like any Type-A/vaguely-OCD pragmatist, I researched the composition of Herbes de Provence: savory, rosemary, thyme, oregano, basil, marjoram, fennel seed. We set off again to the Kroger's. We were able to find dried versions of all except the rosemary, which I yanked off a fresh potted plant in the floral section. Figured I'd use it for garnish. Garnish shows you mean business. Garnish declares your dish isn't just about taste; it's about style. I was styling myself as an elevated autumnal purée for my future family.

At dinner, everyone fussed over my appealing-looking soup. I made a show of walking around to lay a drop of olive oil and a sprig of rosemary in the center of every bowl. I marveled at the fruits of my own tenacity, ignoring the reality that I had just spent over $50 on dried herbs I would never use again.

But then, I noticed my fiancé's mother had pushed her bowl away. Tears welled in her eyes. She said she was sorry but she couldn't eat it. I realized other relatives around the table were having trouble as well. I asked my fiancé what was going on. He had no idea. Finally, my mother-in-law's sister pulled me into the kitchen to explain. "In Cyprus, we plant rosemary bushes at the gravesites of our loved ones. The smell of fresh rosemary makes us think of death—especially our mother's. We lost her to breast cancer in our 20s. She died two months after my sister's wedding. During her honeymoon."

The following Thanksgiving, I brought pie.

Butternut Squash Soup with Herbes de Provence

Adapted from Lorna Sass's
Short-cut Vegetarian; Serves 12.

6 pounds butternut squash
    (cut into 1½-inch chunks)
6 large ribs celery, cut into
    2-inch pieces
2 tablespoons olive oil
4½ cups thinly sliced leeks
12 cups water

4½ tablespoons vegetable stock
1 cup old-fashioned rolled oats
2 tablespoons Herbes de Provence
1½ teaspoons salt
3 tablespoons sherry vinegar
rosemary sprigs, olive oil, and plain
    Greek yogurt for garnish

In a large soup pot, heat 2 table-spoons of oil. Sauté the leeks for about a minute. Add the water and stock and bring to a boil over high heat. Stir in the squash, celery, oats, Herbes de Provence, and salt and return to a boil. Reduce the heat to medium, cover, and cook at a gentle boil until the squash is very soft, about 35–40 minutes.

Purée the soup with an immersion blender. Stir in the vinegar. Garnish with a dot of olive oil, a dollop of Greek yogurt, and a sprig of fresh rosemary—unless you have a Cypriot at the table.

SHEILA CALLAGHAN is a playwright dividing her time between New York and Los Angeles. She is the recipient of a Whiting Award, and was profiled by *Marie Claire* as one of "18 Successful Women Who Are Changing the World." Sheila is currently a writer/producer on the Showtime series *Shameless*.

AIMEE BENDER
ANOTHER STONE SOUP

Because we had no food that day, or only the limp carrots and celery, the sprouted onion, the browning bunch of parsley, I had the children gather stones in the yard. "We will make stone soup," I said, "just like the book." But in the book the villagers have deliciousness to spare, they just do not want to share it. When the children returned with one smooth stone apiece I send them back to find more. I filled the biggest pot with the water I had saved from washing the vegetables on Tuesday, water that was cold from the refrigerator and a pale glowing green. To the children it looked like liquid jade, even though none of us has ever seen jade. They read about it in another book. "It is a beautiful gemstone," said one of the children, nodding. She made sure I caught her eye and agreed. I sent them back for more stones. More.

They finally stood on a stool, one at a time, and dropped each stone into the water as it began to boil, making a tiny splash. I added the chopped carrot and celery with leaves and the onion in its greening circles and all the brown parsley including, I think, the rubber band. "What would be so good with this soup," I said, stirring, "would be a little bit of meat! But it will be fit for a king without it," and the children laughed with delight at the sound of the words from the story and ran outside and returned with handfuls of roly-poly bugs as we had started eating those last week and they are still plentiful plus a few dried up worms from the sandbox. I tossed them into the soup. "Flies?" I said. "What this soup would love is flies!" and off they went again. It is difficult to catch flies but we were getting wilier and we have lots of sticks and nets. It smelled good, it did, and I am sure that the stones added some dirt mineral that we needed because later I told them it was the best stone soup I'd ever had and I meant it.

After a few flies, and some stepped-on bees, and the petals of flowers we had identified as ok, and even the thin snappings of bark from a tree, I did one last stir and let it simmer for forty-five minutes during which the children and I played a few games of "Go Fish," the idea of fish being entirely abstraction by this point. They had gotten so skilled at distracting their hunger but even so at the end H. was throwing himself at the wall as if it were a game and I. and L. were rolling over each other and sticking teeth on the other's arm as if it was a violent kiss but we all knew better.

"Soup!" I said, and they ran in a line and I gave each a cup, a fine cup, our best china, with floral etchings on the side, there was no shortage of those, and I drained the soup and we had about seven cups of a clear broth, and it smelled heavenly. Each child had a cupful and then me too, and then enough for a round two, and I did not have bread but we were lucky enough to find the old broken bits of crackers in a box in the far back of the pantry that some liked to sprinkle in the soup itself. I taught them to say "Bon appétit," which they found very funny. "Once," I said, "people would leave their homes to go into little buildings and read a big card listing lots of foods on it and tell a person what food they would like and that person would then bring it to them, cooked, on a plate!" They loved those stories the best, sipping from their cups with wide eyes and then laughing with amazement. It all seemed so quaint to them.

For dessert, a bit of drawing to make a pie of blue crayon that I carefully cut into many equal slices. "What is blue flavor?" asked J., accepting his, and I said, "sky," to give them a little hope since we still have that, and J. touched his tongue to the paper with care.

AIMEE BENDER is the author of five books, including *The Girl in the Flammable Skirt* and the bestseller *The Particular Sadness of Lemon Cake*. Her short fiction has been published in *Granta, Harper's, The Paris Review, Tin House,* and more, as well as heard on "This American Life" and "Selected Shorts." She lives in Los Angeles and teaches creative writing at USC.

JOY GARNETT
PISS & VINEGAR

There is an old American expression that describes someone brimming with energy whose attitude is slightly salty: they are said to be "full of piss and vinegar." The expression may date as far back as the 1860s and the Pony Express. Riders who ate a full meal and drank plenty of water before heading out were prized. A full stomach and bladder—so went the logic—spurred a rider onward with greater urgency and steely determination.

In 1939, the expression appeared again in John Steinbeck's *The Grapes of Wrath*: "'How ya keepin' yaself?' 'Full a piss an' vinegar,' said Grampa." The novel is set during the Great Depression and tells the story of poor tenant farmers driven from their homes by drought and bank foreclosures. Thousands of "Okies" set out from the Dust Bowl for California seeking land, jobs, and a new life.

For many years, my husband Bill and I lived in an artist's loft in a three-story building on Mercer Street. Our loft was a ramshackle live-work space with a kitchen on one end and our studios in the middle under a big skylight. We made art, cooked, and threw dinner parties.

Then came the Great Recession. Our landlord evicted everyone in our building so they could sell it; we were given a few months to clear out. Bill and I would soon join the ongoing exodus from Manhattan to the boroughs and beyond. That's when I started up a big vat of red wine vinegar in our kitchen-studio. It would take about three months for the wine to ferment. There was just enough time.

I bought some bottles of cheap Bordeaux, purchased the largest glass vat I could carry, and ordered the vinegar mother (*mère de vinaigre*) from a vintner that sold kits for home brewed beer and wine. The vinegar mother is the bacteria starter that converts alcohol to acetic acid—wine to vinegar.

When the movers arrived, everything was packed except for one item: my vat of red wine vinegar. I imagined the large, open-mouthed jar sloshing its smelly, fermenting contents all over the home that we loved and the home that we were still pissed about leaving. But—with greater urgency and steely determination—Bill and I carried the vinegar down to the street, spilling nothing.

Red Wine Vinegar

10 cups red wine
(one 750 milliliter bottle of wine = 3 cups)
2 cups distilled or spring water
(don't use tap water—chlorine will kill the vinegar mother)
1 cup vinegar mother

Homemade red wine vinegar is the most delicious vinegar you will ever taste. Follow this recipe and you will end up with a plentiful supply for use in vinaigrettes, marinades, soups, chutneys, sauces, and stews.

In a 2-gallon open-mouthed earthenware crock, oak barrel, or glass jar, combine the following: 2 cups red wine to begin, plus 8 cups more over the following few weeks, 2 cups distilled or spring water, and 1 cup vinegar mother. Cover the jar with a small square of cheesecloth fastened with string or a rubber band (this will keep the oxygen flowing and the fruit flies out).

Fermentation requires oxygen, warmth, and darkness, so leave the jar in a corner wrapped in a tea towel. In a few weeks, a thin film will appear on the surface. This is the new mother forming. Do not disturb her.

"Feed" the mixture the remaining 8 cups of wine spaced out over the next few weeks. The new vinegar mother may sink whenever you pour in the wine, but don't worry. After two months, the color of the liquid will shift burgundy to reddish-amber. Try it. Mine tastes tart and tawny and deep.

Strain and bottle two thirds of the vinegar, reserving the rest in the jar. Then, open a new bottle of Bordeaux, pour it in, and start a new batch.

JOY GARNETT is an artist and writer who lives in Brooklyn. She has had ten solo exhibitions, and her work has been shown at museums including the Whitney Museum of American Art, MoMA PS1, the Milwaukee Art Museum, and Museum of Contemporary Craft Portland. Garnett writes a column for *Art21 Magazine* and is Arts Editor for *Cultural Politics,* a journal published by Duke University Press. She is the recipient of a grant from Anonymous Was A Woman. Garnett is currently working on a novel.

APRIL GORNIK
DANDELIONS

When I was a child, I'd often see our next-door neighbor out on her lawn in the summer gathering dandelion leaves. I watched her with horror and fascination. Was she a witch, or just eccentric? Who in their right mind would eat dandelions?

Then one Saturday a few years ago at my local CSA, someone pointed to a weed that I had seen many times before and said enthusiastically, "That's purslane. Did you know it has more nutritional value than almost anything else in your garden?" I tasted it—lemony and mild with a great texture—and of course rushed home and googled it.

The first things that came up were toxic products to remove it as a noxious weed. But, after more searching,

I found out that it's higher in Omega-3 than anything else in the vegetable kingdom, even higher than in many kinds of fish oil, that it's a powerful antioxidant, and is also an excellent source of vitamin A. Thus began my fascination with "weeds" and their potential to be not only delicious foods, but also sources of nutrition.

Which brings me back to dandelions. Fifty years later, and I've become that lady next door who I watched with horror and fascination as a child. You can often find me in my organic, non-treated garden, or on my lawn, and other people's lawns, and wherever I can find them, foraging away like a crazed organic enthusiast for dandelion greens. They have powerful health benefits, including vitamin A, potassium, calcium, and vitamin

K, with a deliciously zingy and slightly bitter taste that combines beautifully with a slightly sweet salad dressing. A daily pleasure for me is fresh-picked dandelion greens and purslane, chopped, dressed, and topped with an egg. It's super-nutritious comfort food.

Chopped Dandelion and Purslane Salad

dandelion greens and purslane, chopped
3 tablespoons fig vinegar (I love Vincotto brand fig vinegar)
⅓–½ cup extra-virgin orange-flavored olive oil (Arlotta Food Studio's blood orange infused olive oil is divine!)
a splash of colatura (an Italian anchovy sauce sold in specialty stores that's similar to Thai fish sauce, and equally smelly, but you only use a few drops)
1 teaspoon good mustard (optional)
1 organic egg
sea salt and pepper to taste

Chop greens. Mix all other ingredients except egg. Then, cook a delicious farm-raised organic egg sunny side up, toss the dandelions and purslane with the dressing, season with sea salt and pepper, top with the egg and serve.

APRIL GORNIK is an artist living and working in Sag Harbor, New York. She has work in the Metropolitan Museum of Art, the Whitney Museum of American Art, the Museum of Modern Art, the National Museum of American Art in Washington, DC, and other major public and private collections. She has shown extensively, in one-person and group shows, in the United States and abroad.

KATE CHRISTENSEN
DAYDREAMER'S SALAD

All my life, I've done a lot of daydreaming, otherwise known as woolgathering, fantasizing, and spacing out. It's one of my favorite hobbies, along with eating. It's free and portable and available to anyone, anytime. You don't need any equipment or training. All you have to do is ignore whatever's right in front of you and let your mind go wherever it wants. There are no rules, no one is watching, and nothing is off-limits. It's one of the few absolute, eternal freedoms we possess.

The best daydreams are the ones that erase the present and feel so real it's almost as if they've become true through sheer force of imagination: the transporting ones, the ones that give the daydreamer something like a temporary parallel existence.

In mid morning today, staring at a blank computer screen with a sense of dread, feeling the stresses of adult life and unwilling to contend with any of it, I rowed off in my mind across a vast, quiet lake in a canoe with a huge picnic basket, a canvas tarp, and an old-fashioned zippered sleeping bag.

I was 11, with my imaginary childhood best friend. Simultaneously, I was 14, with my imaginary summer boyfriend, sneaking away from our families for an afternoon. Also at the same time, Brendan was paddling in synch with me, Dingo sitting between us, his big bat ears peaked in the lake breeze. But really, I was alone in the absolute quiet.

After a long time, I came to a piney, rocky island in the center of the lake, isolated and far from any sign of people. I landed the canoe and carried everything ashore. I strung a rope between two trees and slung the tarp over it and weighted it with rocks, and then I unrolled my sleeping bag inside.

After I wedged the picnic basket in the roots and shade of a huge tree, I stripped and dove into the clean, cold water. And then, ravenous after a long, hard swim, I sat on the edge of the island, looking out over the water, and opened my picnic basket.

This was the best part of the daydream, the high point,

and the purpose. In the hamper was a carefully curated picnic, one that took me a while to come up with as I stared into space, choosing, rejecting, and adding. In the end, I brought half a cold, roast rosemary-and-lemon chicken, a container of vinegary German potato salad, a sourdough roll, dusty with fine flour—I can eat all the gluten I want in my daydreams—and a mild, buttery brie, an aged Gouda, herbed mixed olives, a salami, and cornichons. I also had a container of raw vegetables: sliced cucumber, red pepper, radishes, and celery. And a bottle of Côtes du Rhône, slightly chilled.

For dessert, I had a sack of fresh-picked wild blueberries, a bar of hazelnut bittersweet chocolate, and a big thermos of tart, fresh lemonade, crackling with little ice cubes.

After I'd glutted myself, I sacked out in my canvas lean-to on my sleeping bag with the shadows of pine branches making patterns on my eyelids. A sweet-smelling breeze lifted the tarp gently and let it go again, without making a sound, as if I were inside a healthy lung. Dragonflies helicoptered through the air with a soporific buzz. The pine needles gave off their perfume. The pine boughs lifted and sank with a hushing sound.

I got chilly after a while and burrowed into my bag without waking up. The soft flannel inside smelled of long-ago campfires and past summers. The taste of the chicken and cheese and salami stayed on my tongue while I slept. When I woke up from this epic nap, I drank a bellyful of lemonade and dove into the lake again, and then, while the shadows got longer and the air cooled, I packed everything into the canoe and paddled for a long, calm, quiet hour back home.

When I got back, my computer screen was there in front of me, still empty, along with every damned thing I was worried about. Also, I was hungry. From the fridge, I fetched the rest of the purple cabbage, three carrots, and a head of greenleaf lettuce. With a red onion and a can of smoked kippers, I made a lunch so simple but good, it almost made me forget the imagined one.

Kipper Salad

green leaf lettuce
red onion
smoked kippers
mayonnaise
lemon

Wash and tear into small bits 10 tender, fresh leaves of greenleaf lettuce.

Thinly slice ½ red onion.

Open a can of Bar Harbor peppered smoked kippers.

Toss all ingredients with the following dressing: the liquid from the tinned fish, a dollop of mayonnaise, and the juice of ¼ lemon.

Serve alongside a crisp coleslaw.

Coleslaw

purple cabbage
carrots
mayonnaise
mustard
salt and black pepper
sugar
apple vinegar

Grate the cabbage and carrots, and then lightly dress it with a mixture of mayonnaise, mustard, salt and black pepper, sugar, and apple vinegar.

KATE CHRISTENSEN is the author of seven novels, including *The Great Man*, which won the 2008 PEN/ Faulkner Award for Fiction, and the forthcoming *The Last Cruise*. She has also published two food-centric memoirs, *Blue Plate Special* and *How to Cook a Moose*.

ZHANG HUAN
FO TIAO QIANG, OR
BUDDHA JUMPS OVER THE WALL

About ten years ago, I started practicing Buddhism at home and going to temple regularly to worship. Once, in the temple I go to most often, I was introduced to a wonderful soup called Fo Tiao Qiang, or Buddha Jumps over the Wall. I asked why it was given this unusual name, and here is the story I was told.

About 100 years ago, in the Qing Dynasty, a group of beggars took their pots around, asking for food. Afterwards, they gathered what they had each received and cooked it all together. The fragrance was so delicious that the Buddhist monks, meditating in the nearby temple, couldn't resist; they jumped over the wall and gorged.

The original Fo Tiao Qiang, or Buddha Jumps over the Wall, is cooked with meat and vegetables. In my temple, though, I was introduced to a vegetarian version. It is truly scrumptious; I'll never forget how I felt when I first tasted it. And while I didn't have to jump over any walls to try it, I agree: It's worth it.

Fo Tiao Qiang

4 Chinese mushrooms, sliced
½ pound bean sprouts
½ pound corn, cut into segments
½ pound bamboo shoots, peeled and cut into pieces
½ pound wax gourds, peeled and cut into pieces
½ pound Chinese cabbage, sliced
½ pound bean vermicelli, chopped
½ pound green soybeans
1 teaspoons salt
Chinese yam or taro, sliced (optional)
vinegar (optional)
soy sauce (optional)

Prepare a vegetable stock in a big pot. It can be store-bought, or you can make the stock yourself: Add Chinese mushrooms, bean sprouts, and corn into a big pot with water. Add no seasoning in this process. Simmer for two hours. Remove the vegetables from the pot.

Then, take a casserole dish. Add bamboo shoots, wax gourds, and Chinese cabbage along the edges of the dish so that they form a circle. Add the prepared vegetable stock no higher than the level of the vegetables. Cover, bring to a boil, then turn down the flame and steam for about one hour.

Add salt just before turning off the fire.

Lastly: Stir-fry the boiled corn kernels with green soybeans and add a pinch of salt. Place them on top of the pot, stir and serve. If you feel this dish is too light, add some vinegar and soy sauce to taste.

ZHANG HUAN is an artist who was born in 1965 in Anyang City, Henan Province. He subsequently lived and worked in New York City where he gained international recognition. Zhang Huan has had solo exhibitions at museums including the Norton Museum of Art, the Shanghai Art Museum, and the Art Gallery of Ontario, and has been featured in group exhibitions at museum including the Guggenheim and the Whitney. He is the first Chinese modern artist to direct a lyric opera. In 2014, Zhang Huan was awarded Chevalier de la Légion d'Honneur by the French government.

SANDWICHES
&
PIZZA

DANIEL WALLACE
Love AND EGGPLANT

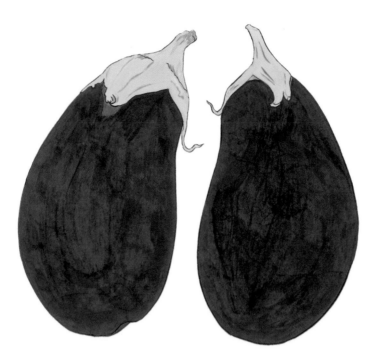

Never woo a woman with an eggplant: I think it was Shakespeare or Margaret Thatcher who said that. And yet I tried, and it was a mistake made for two reasons, only one of them true. Eggplant, I could say, is a species of nightshade, and nightshade is a beautiful word, suggestive of romance. Think of it: a union so intimate that not only must the *light* be shaded, but so too the night. Eggplant speaks the language of love.

But that's not true. The real reason is that it was the only food I knew how to make. I have learned some new tricks since then, but 15 years ago I didn't bring much magic to the kitchen. I could boil water and I could do it in three different ways. I could boil water for the dropping of spaghetti into it; I could boil water, cover the pan with a top and steam broccoli; and I could boil water and with it make coffee or tea—the trifecta, in other words. But after my first marriage crumbled for reasons unrelated to food and hot water, I learned to do something else.

I learned to make an eggplant sandwich.

I don't know why this happened, why I made this instead of something that did not involve eggplant. It was open-faced, and it included pesto and cheese, and I made it for myself a number of times before serving it to the woman I hoped to woo. I was confident; I'd thought things through. A sandwich, I figured, was too casual for dinner. But an open-faced sandwich brought a level of fancy to the dish, and begs the question as to whether it's a sandwich at all. Also, there was the eggplant. Eggplant could not have been more exotic to me. Surely Laura would feel the same. She would appreciate my knowledge of this rare and possibly dangerous fruit.

So I served it, and Laura ate it, and some years later we were married.

She didn't say much at the time. Months passed before she told me how she much she truly hated it, what a *erreur de la cuisine* it was—but this sort of hiatus between an event and the truth behind the event was, or would become, the way we were. A similar thing happened the night we first met. I was at a bar; she was the bartender. It was a quiet night and I'd just published my first book, and after bringing me a gin and tonic she asked—apropos of nothing, it seemed—if I were a writer. I said yes. *I thought so,* she said. She left, served two guys at the other end of the bar and came back. *Are you . . . Daniel Wallace?* I nodded. *You wrote* Big Fish, *right?*

This was the first time I'd been recognized outside of my immediate family as being a writer. There is no faster acting aphrodisiac than this. She was beautiful, she was a bartender, and she read *The New York Times Book Review.* I just described the perfect woman.

It was only later, after I'd fallen too deeply in love with her to care, that she told me she did not read the *Book Review,* and would have had no idea who I was had it not been for the two guys at the end of the bar, who did read the *Book Review* and who had seen me on the elliptical at the gym.

But that's another story; this one is about love and eggplant. Although we've been married 14 years and I've made a lot of dinners—I have skillz now, real skillz—I have not been asked to make that sandwich again, for old time's or any sake at all. In fact, I have been told expressly not to. I haven't even made it for myself since then. It's a sandwich from a different time in my life, one I have no desire to re-visit now. But here it is. A simple recipe, but how could it not be?

Eggplant Sandwich

1 baguette
pesto
cheddar cheese
garlic cloves, minced

Cut your baguette in half horizontally. Smear as much pesto as you want to across it.

Place the eggplant, cut into medallions, on top of the pesto, and cheddar cheese on top of the eggplant, then garlic cloves, minced and liberally distributed across the top.

Bake at 350 until the cheese bubbles, and you're done. Or not. Depending on the woman.

DANIEL WALLACE is author of five novels that have been translated into over two-dozen languages, including *Big Fish* and *The Kings and Queens of Roam.* In 2003, *Big Fish* was adapted and released as a movie, and then in 2013, the book and the movie were mish-mashed into a Broadway musical. Daniel Wallace is the J. Ross MacDonald Distinguished Professor of English at the University of North Carolina at Chapel Hill, his alma mater, where he directs the Creative Writing Program. He lives in Chapel Hill with his wife, Laura Kellison Wallace.

JAMES FRANCO
THE UTILITARIAN, AMERICAN-STYLE PB&J: AN ARTIST'S BEST FRIEND

I don't remember my mother cooking much when I was young. She did cook a meal every night, but my favorite was always Thursday nights when she would lay out sandwich fixings with some nice French bread, that was the special meal. And hell, I can't blame her for not spending time on the cooking; she was raising three boys while still finding time to write her books.

My mom never made me eat school lunches at elementary school. I was spared the Sloppy Joes and scary looking meat in the hot lunch tins; instead I got the same thing every day: a peanut butter and jelly sandwich on wheat bread. It was a simple and dependable meal (with an apple and a Sunkist Juice Squeeze) that I could down quickly, in order to use the maximum amount of the lunch break to play dodgeball or handball.

The PB&Js continued into junior high (they sold pizza on campus, but it was greasy as shit) and then into high school. I was given lunch money but in high school I saved this in order to buy alcohol on the weekends. My mother kept making those PB&Js.

Now I work on movie sets. Depending on the size of the movie, the level of snacks can range from a few bags of Doritos and a bowl of carrots to tables full of soups, fine breads, chocolates, candies, and crudités. I am usually content with a PB&J. It is simple and safe and keeps me going. On a movie a PB&J is usually good around 11 a.m., around the time you've put in some good work on the first scene. You might think that it will ruin your lunch, but it can actually serve as a pre-lunch. I actually don't eat a ton on movie sets, and I usually don't trust the meat (a hold over from the Sloppy Joes?), so I'm a vegetarian on movie sets, and a confirmed PB&J lover. I think they go along with my mother's utilitarian/artistic nature. It's about the work, so don't let your food take time away from your writing or acting or filmmaking or whatever. A PB&J is the perfect thing to hold while you're doing other things.

Nothing like a PB&J. It is sweet and savory. The fluffy bread keeps the sticky stuff in check, and it all goes down well with a soda. I stopped drinking Diet Coke because of all the chemicals in it, so I drink Ginger Ale. Just thinking about a PB&J and a familiar can of Canada Dry Ginger Ale is making me hungry.

Sometimes I even put a pickle on the side. NOT IN the sandwich, just on the side to give a little sour/salty tang to the sweet and savory mix already going on in the sandwich.

PB&J

wheat bread
peanut butter
jelly
ginger ale (optional)
pickles (optional)

Bread – Two slices of wheat bread.

Not too thick.

You can also lightly toast the bread, but not too dark, you want a soft sandwich to absorb the jelly, if it's too hard the fixings will slide out the sides.

Peanut butter – The key here is the right amount. It should be balanced with the jelly content so that neither one overpowers the other.

It can be chunky or smooth depending on your preference.

Some people like to switch this ingredient out for almond butter or Nutella or some such crap, but I'm a down to basics, American kind of guy when it comes to my PB&Js. My preference for wheat bread over white might betray a bit of European pizazz, but that's where such flashiness ends. A PB&J needs the *PB* or it ain't a *PB AND J!*

Jelly – I'm partial to the berries: strawberry, raspberry, or grape. I think apricot/orange do not go well with the peanut butter. Go with the reds and purples and stay away from the orange colored jellies.

Optional Additions:

Ginger ale – Canada Dry is my preferred choice here because it reminds me of picnics on the beach with my family. But most drinks will go with a PB&J: black coffee, bottled water, Sprite, or even the old classic, a glass of milk.

Pickle – This is my thang. Do not put this in the sandwich. Some people put bananas or potato chips in their PB&Js but those are not PB&Js, those are mutations. But a pickle on the side gives a tang of sophistication, a good palate cleanser.

Get to work, suckas.

JAMES FRANCO is an actor, director, artist, and writer. His film appearances include *Milk, Pineapple Express, Eat, Pray, Love, Howl,* and *127 Hours,* which earned him an Academy Award nomination. He is the author of books including the novel *Actors Anonymous,* the collection *Palo Alto,* and the memoir *A California Childhood.* His writing has been published in *Esquire, Vanity Fair, N+1, The Wall Street Journal,* and *McSweeney's;* his art has been exhibited throughout the world including at the Museum of Contemporary Art in Los Angeles and Deitch Projects in New York.

AMBER DERMONT
LOBSTER ROLLS

As a daughter/chef who was raised to please/feed her parents, I can say with authority that nothing makes my mother happier than a lobster roll. Okay, maybe a Scotch Old-Fashioned or an afternoon with her grandchildren, but a lobster roll is her madeleine, a delicious memory of childhood summers on Cape Cod. Make Mom a lobster roll and the world is your oyster—she'll do anything for you. This adoration goes so deep that my parents raised our family in New England just to honor my mother's love for crustaceans.

Growing up I could walk to the beach, swim out to the kelp beds, dig for scallops and clams with my toes, then pry mussels off rocks and take my bounty home for bouillabaisse. As an adult, I've dined in some of the world's most celebrated white-linen restaurants, but, for my money, there is nothing better than a table spread with newspapers awaiting a spilled pot of steamed shellfish. This is my perfect culinary storm.

With apologies to the late David Foster Wallace: Consider the Lobster Roll. The sublime marriage of salty sweetness, creamy mayo, toasted buttery bun. A lobster roll is summertime. It's the only sandwich that is also a vacation. Lobster rolls are best consumed on a crowded picnic bench with a fish shack-view of yachts and circling seagulls—the pinnacle of comfort and pretension. Simple and divine, it will cost you a small fortune and it's worth it.

Cooking a lobster, however, is ethically unsound. Be advised that you are committing an act of oceanic terrorism. Lobsters feel pain—though what sort of pain is unclear. According to Trevor Corson's *The Secret Lives of Lobsters,* these wild creatures are always ready to rumble, rarely blink when they lose a limb in battle and enjoy pissing in their opponents faces (their bladders are on their heads). Maybe lobsters are assholes. Maybe they have that steam pot coming to them.

Although lobsters don't actually mate for life (sorry Phoebe Buffay), male lobsters do have two penises. Lobsters participate in ritualistic courtships with choreographed dance routines. The females go shell-less when engaging in sex. They must feel something: the agony and the ecstasy of the sea. If allowed to roam, a wild lobster will live forever or at least as long as my grandmother, Stella. Make no mistake, a lobster will fight an enemy to the death, tear their own shells off when it's time to molt (literally with their bare claws) and protect their homes from invaders both foreign and domestic. Maybe lobsters aren't assholes. Maybe they're just patriotic. Perhaps the author Gerard de Nerval understood lobsters best when, in defiance of protocol, he paraded his own pet lobster, Thibault, through the gardens of Paris on a blue silk leash.

If I could, I would buy all of the lobsters their own blue silk ribbons but my mother demands a sacrifice. And, if you want a lobster roll, you're going to have to cook some lobsters. Here's a secret to finding a willing volunteer: Sometimes, when you go to the fish market and stare long enough at the lobster aquariums—those gurgling purgatories of despair—you get lucky. One of the lobsters will frantically wave a claw and signal that he is yours. Take him up on his offer. It's crowded in that tank.

Some diners are size queens and go for those big five-pound numbers. Let the foolish investment bankers choke on their rubbery meat. Those giant lobsters are ancient. What you want for your lobster roll is a small 1 ¼–1 ½ pound lobster—buy three if you wish to share. The meat from the younger, smaller lobsters will be tender and succulent.

Obviously, you want Maine lobsters. Those critters from Florida or Australia are just spiny cockroaches with claws. Never buy lobster meat that has already been cooked. Always buy live lobsters. Always from Maine. Lobstermen are some of the greatest people in the world and they deserve our adoration and patronage.

Lobster Rolls

3 lobsters, 1¼–1½ pounds
mayonnaise to taste
lemon to taste
salt to taste
black pepper to taste
6 New England hot dog buns
butter
chopped chives (purely ornamental and entirely unnecessary)

To prepare the lobsters, you don't need to boil a roiling bucket of water. Lobsters should be steamed. Just pour a few inches of water into a pot, add sea salt, place a steamer rack on the bottom of the pot, cut a lemon in half and toss that in too. Let the water boil, then add your lobsters (either live or use the old quick-sharp-knife-to-the-head method).

While you are waiting for the lobsters to steam, make a Scotch Old-Fashioned. By the time you're done, the lobsters should be bright red (8-10 minutes for the first pound then 4 minutes for each additional pound). Some people recommend tugging on the lobster's antennae to see if they are done. These people are sadists.

Remove the lobsters from the pot and allow them to cool. I can crack a lobster's shell with my bare hands, remove the flesh and then perfectly reconstruct the lobster sans shell. I have tiny hands but they work better than any of those metallic cracker torture devices. The lobster chose you. You owe it to the lobster to disassemble him by hand. If you aren't brave enough to do this, crack away but be gentle. You don't want to crush the lobster meat. Don't add anything else to the meat just yet. Cover and refrigerate.

As the lobster meat chills, take the time to fly to New England and buy a bag of hotdog buns. These buns are unlike any other buns in the world. Invented by J.J. Nissen just after World War II, these buns are toploaders: split in the middle with bare sides perfect for buttering and toasting. Lots of beautiful lobster meat has been destroyed by hard

→

torpedo rolls. Don't let this happen to yours. You want a soft-on-the-inside yeasty bread. Toast the sides of the buns in plenty of butter until they are golden brown. Don't burn the buns and don't skimp on the butter.

Now, there are competing schools of thought as to what constitutes the filling of a lobster roll. Some people like to serve their lobster warm and dripping in drawn butter. Some like to go the lobster salad route and add celery, lettuce, tomatoes, onions and parsley. Others like to add mango and cilantro. All of these people are wrong. If you know someone who adds tarragon or scallions to their lobster roll, stop being friends with this person immediately. You are welcome to chop some chives and sprinkle them on top of the lobster roll before serving if you think the bright green contrast will look pretty against the red/white meat but this is not a Martha Stewart Living photo shoot, this is serious business. The chives may add to the beauty but will detract from the taste of the lobster. Onions, garlic, celery are all to be avoided. Trust the lobster to do the work of the lobster roll.

The beauty of this dish is that you simply need to squeeze fresh lemon for brightness and add chilled mayonnaise to the lobster meat. Place the mixture gently in the cradle of the toasted New England hotdog bun. Some people like to make fresh aioli but Hellmann's is delicious and has been served in America since 1905, so show some respect. If you prefer Duke's or Best you are welcome to use those brands. The point of the mayo is to enhance the relationship between the lobster and the bread. Add as much or as little mayonnaise as you like, just do not skimp on the lobster meat. Use the body, the knuckles and the claws. There is nothing worse than a lobster roll that is just claw-tip meat. Roughly chop or gently tear the lobster meat but leave the claws intact. Season if you like, but if the meat is delicious there is no need for salt or black pepper. The combination of chilled lobster meat and warm bun will heighten all of your senses. Take a bite. My mother thanks you.

AMBER DERMONT is the author of *The New York Times* bestselling novel, *The Starboard Sea* and the short story collection, *Damage Control.* A graduate of the Iowa Writers' Workshop, she is the recipient of fellowships from the National Endowment for the Arts, the Bread Loaf Writers' Conference and the Sewanee Writers' Conference. Amber Dermont lives in Houston, Texas where she is an Associate Professor of English and Creative Writing at Rice University.

JAMES SIENA
THE CRUST

To me, the holy grail of good pizza is the crust. Thirty-five years ago, I made it my mission to master the living crust that, despite its death by oven, sustains us all. And to this day, whenever I make pizza, I learn a little more about that simple thing, which, at the first impression, is all about the crust.

It began at Round Table Pizza on El Camino in Menlo Park, California back in the 60s and 70s, where you would find little Jimmy Siena eating everyone's leftover crusts smeared with faint stains of tomato, to the occasional consternation of neighboring diners. My parents loved to take us when my father was in Law School at Stanford in '61–62. We returned as a family of five in '69, and lo and behold, Round Table had endured, complete with the only (at the time) concession of Anchor Steam Beer. (Yes, I was too young, but not too young to dream.) Eventually, though, Round Table went on to become a chain of pizza franchises all over Northern California, where the love was absent, the crust mediocre, and the toppings prevailed. It was loud and

vulgar, and I longed, in my adolescence, for the old place on El Camino, with the unavailable (to me) Anchor Steam.

Anyway, my time in the Bay Area would come to an end in '75. I went east, to Cornell. I did a lot of cooking there, and began baking bread regularly. After getting my degree I ended up living in a terminally funky country house outside of Ithaca, N.Y. My rent: $45 per month, with a hand pump for water out back. We used a lot of buckets. Heat was provided, sparingly, by a couple of woodstoves. Hot water was provided by a gigantic, 30-inch-tall kettle that sat on one of the stoves, but despite our best efforts, bedrooms were below freezing in winter. One way to keep warm was to cook a lot in a small kitchen whose old stove used both gas and wood. When I noticed the oven could get up to 700 degrees, I started making pizzas.

A couple of years later, in search of running water, heat, and flush toilets, I moved to New York, and in '88, my son Joe Siena was born to my then-wife Iris Rose. Around that time, I initiated a tradition of making pizza on Thursday

→

nights. With my parents no longer alive, I somehow tied pizza to filial cohesion; our table became Round Table. Hundreds of pizzas passed out of that oven on Broome Street on the Lower East Side in the 90s and early aughts. Thursday mornings were hectic: I'd prepare a big batch of dough while Joe was getting ready for school and let it rise all day, then pick up fresh mozzarella at DiPalo's on Grand Street on our way home.

Joe lives in Queens now, and we don't do pizza night on Thursdays anymore (he oversees an open mic night in the West Village those nights). But sometimes when he comes up to our country place in Otis, Massachusetts we fire up a much more modern oven and turn out some pies. And, unlike at Round Table, the crusts are devoured by everyone.

James Siena's Pizza

Pizza Dough

1 palmful yeast
1 palmful sugar
1 palmful salt
4 cups warm, but not hot, water
flour (I've never measured, but
    5 pounds should be more than
    enough)
olive oil
coarse cornmeal

With a wire whisk, dissolve the yeast, salt, and sugar in the warm water. Use a large bowl, the largest in your kitchen. Add 2 or 3 cups of flour, also using the whisk. Let the mixture rest, and the yeast activate, for an hour or two (this step can be skipped, but the texture and flavor and life of the dough will be more vital if you don't).

When you resume adding flour, you should see a foam or sponge on the surface of the mixture. Continue adding flour using the whisk until the whisk starts to get clogged. Let the mixture rest again about an hour. Add more flour, slowly, using a wooden spoon or spatula, taking care to keep the dough a little bit sticky and wet. Turn the dough out of the bowl onto a floured board, clean the bowl, pour in some olive oil, and return the dough to the bowl. Cover the bowl with a cookie sheet or anything else that spans the whole top of the bowl (a towel can span the gaps if needs be, but don't just use a towel, as it will sag and stick to the dough), and

let the dough rise for an hour or two. A good place to do this is in an oven whose pilot light is sufficient to make a warm place. Punch it down and let it rise again.

You are now ready to make the pizzas. I like dough that has been sitting around a while (up to a day in the kitchen, lightly covered, or up to a week in the fridge, though be sure that the dough gets air or it will die), but this my personal preference. You can also freeze the dough for months, which is convenient, especially if you double the recipe.

I don't believe in pizza stones. I love cast iron, but if I'm making a mess of pizzas, I'll use any flat bottomed frying pan. So, sprinkle the coarse cornmeal onto some frying pans. Place a pile of flour at one end of the cutting board and spread a good thick layer across it. Pull up a ball of dough out of the bowl and pinch it off; it should be about the size of a fist, maybe a bit larger for a griddle-sized pizza. Place it on the floured board and spread it out slowly. If you like round pizzas, do this carefully; I have never obsessed about this, so my pizzas are irregular. Your hands will get completely doughy, so just make sure you are getting flour on your fingers to help you manage the dough. Try to make the dough less than ¼-inch thick. It's legal to roll it out a bit, too, if that will help.

Once you have a shape ready to put

in a pan, flour it a little on the top and fold it twice. Carry it to the pan and unfold it. This method prevents tearing. Repeat the process for as many pizzas as you are making; the toppings can wait.

Pizza Toppings
(all optional, except mozzarella)

tomato sauce
capers
anchovies
black olives
fresh mozzarella
Parmesan, grated

Lou DiPalo recommends refrigerating the mozzarella for a day or two to let the butterfat be absorbed into the cheese. I concur. I also like older mozzarella, and freeze it up in the country, as it's not that easy to find up there. But it performs well under all these conditions. Slice it about ¼-inch thick, and press it between paper towels, using cutting boards and weight (a gallon of water is heavy enough). Let it sit there for half an hour.

I like to put the onions down first, then the cheese, then capers, olives, and anchovies (be sure to drizzle some oil from the can if you use anchovies). If you like tomato sauce, put that down first, but sparingly, spreading it with the back of a large spoon. Other toppings that perform well and get deliciously crispy and concentrated in flavor are ham, prosciutto, and smoked salmon. These things shrink and sometimes burn a little, which I love.

I recommend baking at 500 degrees, higher if possible. Bake the pizzas until the crust turns a bit darker and starts to curl away at the edges from the pan, or until the cheese starts to brown. If you have any trouble getting your oven hot enough, raise the rack as high as you can.

Finally, grate some Parmesan just before putting the pizzas in the oven. It's also good, of course, to grate some more after serving.

JAMES SIENA works across media exploring the range of possibilities that result when handmade or analog processes are executed with systematic constraints. Celebrated for the brightly colored enamel on aluminum paintings he has made since the early 1990s, Siena also produces engravings, etchings, lithographs, woodcuts, drawings executed on typewriters, and sculptures. He has been featured in more than one hundred solo and group exhibitions since 1981.

JANE SMILEY
TRENTON TOMATO PIE

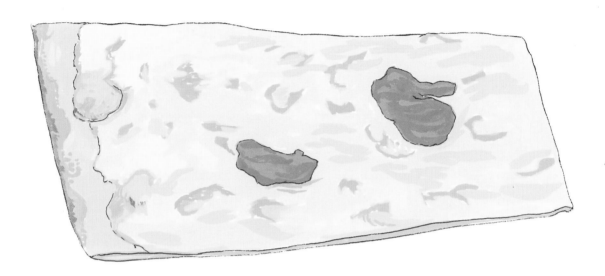

As long as I've known him, my husband, who is from Philadephia, has been talking about the foods he left behind. Although he has not won me over to scrapple or Taylor Pork Roll, and you simply cannot make a Philly Cheese Steak in California, we have spent years refining this Trenton, New Jersey pizza. In Trenton, they will tell you that pizza was actually invented in a steel mill in a town near Trenton and exported to Naples, although it's not actually called "pizza" in Trenton, it's called "Tomato Pie."

We eat TTP once a week, usually on Mondays. Over the years, I have trickled in a few of my own ideas, like making the crust with half white whole wheat flour and half 00 pasta flour from Italy. I don't know where Trenton gets its flour. I also prefer to make the dough a few days ahead of time, divide it into three sections, pat each one into a little circle, and then freeze them—the crust is more bubbly and crispier after freezing. A few toppings are better than too many. It is very important to cut the pie crosswise rather than into wedges. I do not know why.

For years, my husband has talked about De Lorenzo's Tomato Pie, so a few months ago, when we were back in the east, we went looking for one. His favorite De Lorenzo's used to be on Hamilton Avenue, in Trenton, but it closed, allegedly because for safety's sake, customers had to be accompanied to their cars after eating there. The one we went to was in Robbinsville. We were disappointed—too much tomato, cheese not on first. And, the next day, we could barely eat the Philly Cheese Steak. When we got back to California, we made our own pie and enjoyed it, and so I decided that it is not a sign of grumpy old age, but a sign that we have learned just exactly how to please ourselves.

Jane and Jack's Trenton Tomato Pie, Carmel version

1 cup Italian flour
1 cup white whole wheat flour
1 teaspoon instant yeast
½ teaspoon salt
1 cup warm water
2 tablespoons olive oil
a sprinkle of corn meal

Put the dry ingredients in the food processor and process for a few seconds. Slowly add water and olive oil; process until a loose ball is formed. Let this sit in the food processor for a couple of hours until it rises to about double in size.

When you are ready to cook the pie, put the stone in the oven and preheat to 450.

Process the dough for a second or two, then remove from the food processor and knead enough flour into it (maybe a small handful) to make it workable and not sticky. Divide into three parts. You have enough for three pies. If you want to make only one, flatten the other two parts, put in a plastic bag, and freeze (the crust is actually better after freezing and thawing). Using a little more flour, roll out the crust to a circle about 9 or 10 inches in diameter. Let it rest while you prepare the toppings.

Pizza Toppings

2 ounces + of Parmesan cheese, grated
3 ounces + of mozzarella cheese, grated
stewed canned Italian tomatoes

Optional: We like bacon (be sure to precook), onion, chopped garlic, basil, pesto, anchovies, sun-dried tomatoes, sweet red pepper, ham, mushrooms, mix and match, everything sliced very thin.

Sprinkle corn meal on the pizza paddle, roll the crust just a little thinner, and ease it onto the paddle. Shake the paddle a little to make sure that the crust slides back and forth.

Put the cheeses on first, then the chopped garlic, then the other toppings that you have chosen. Three or four is best, because the crust is thin. Tomatoes go on last. Drain the can; squeeze some tomatoes between your fingers and distribute them over the pie. More or less, as you desire. Often, we substitute sun dried tomatoes for the stewed ones. Sprinkle with Italian seasoning and seasoned pepper, then a few thin swirls of olive oil. When you have finished putting on the toppings, shake the paddle a little to see if the crust is still sliding.

Open the oven, and slide the pizza off the paddle onto the stone. If it sticks a little, ease the edge of a metal spatula around the edge of the crust. You want it to slip down on its own and come to rest on the stone. If you must use the spatula, pulling it down a little is better than trying to push it—the crust has elasticity, but no substance.

Cook for 9 minutes.

When the pizza is done, the cheese should be melted, the crust crisp and brown and a little puffed here and there. Using the paddle, take it out of the oven, and place on a cold surface (like tiles) for a minute or so. Move to cutting board, and cut up with pizza slicer. The crust should be so crisp that it sticks straight out when you hold it by the edge.

If there are leftovers, you can place the slices in a cold skillet, turn on the burner and simply heat them up. They are thin, so they heat up very quickly.

JANE SMILEY is the author of many novels and works of non-fiction, including her best-selling novel *A Thousand Acres,* a story based on William Shakespeare's *King Lear,* which received the Pulitzer Prize for Fiction in 1992 and was adapted into a film in 1997. The third volume of her "Last Hundred Years" trilogy, *Golden Age,* was published in the fall of 2015. She lives in California, and is a perfect example to all parents that there is hope even for the pickiest of eaters.

NICKY BEER
KENTUCKY PIZZA

In grad school, neither my husband nor I had much cooking skill—I'm sure the culinary equivalent of the ASPCA would want me to answer for the things I did to eggs—and our diet consisted of take-out, Old El Paso Taco dinner kits, and instant mac-n-cheese. Like most impoverished twentysomethings, we treated pizza as a food group unto itself. While studying at the University of Houston, we regularly devoured spinach pies from Star Pizza, washing them down with Shiner. When we needed cheaper and faster fare, we got Papa John's. At Mizzou, we worshipped the venerated Shakespeare's Pizza, and even though the stoned delivery guys frequently went AWOL en route to our house, we still kept in touch with Papa J's.

All of this changed when my husband got his first tenure-track job at Murray State University. Murray is a town in rural western Kentucky, close to the Tennessee border. We moved into a sprawling ranch house rental "out in the county," about a 15-minute drive from town. We were surrounded by verdant farmland—soy, corn, and tobacco fields. We'd sit out in the backyard acre and read and write under the shade of a massive oak tree, the neighbor's horses grazing nearby as the sun glossed their flanks. For hours, the only sound would be the wind pushing through the leaves. At dusk, the sun would sink down behind the pasture in smeary drapes of orange and purple, and we'd hear frogs sing in the marsh, while bats shuddered across the sky. We had privacy, peace, and an intimacy with the natural world like we'd never known before.

And: no pizza delivery.

As far removed from town as we were, even Domino's wouldn't deign to make the drive out. This proved to be something of a crisis; we were already coping with living in a dry county, the inescapability of Wal-Mart, and the fact that the university health plan didn't cover my birth control. *But goddammit, we needed our goddamned pizza, goddammit.*

Could I, the queen of taco kits, defiler of eggs, actually learn how to make my own pizza? After a couple of timid internet searches, I found a recipe I could work with. Aside from some Lucy-esque physical comedy while kneading, the entire process of crust-making turned out to be fairly simple: mix a bunch of stuff together, make sure the water is at the right temperature, then leave it the hell alone. I will never forget the shock when, after about 90 minutes, I discovered the dough had *done exactly what the recipe said it would.* It changed! It was larger and spongy-looking! And it was because I did something right!

I covered the dough in a jarred sauce, mozzarella, and some sautéed zucchini, stuck it in the oven on a pizza stone, and was again astonished when what came out looked like pizza, and even tasted like pizza. I was happy. My husband was happy. We were now the masters of our own pizza destiny.

I've been making pizza for about seven years now. Even though my husband and I have relocated to Denver, which has oodles of excellent pizza establishments, homemade pizza is still part of our regular dinner rotation. I'm especially sentimental about this recipe because it's become a reflection of the small ways in which I've become a better cook, and have developed enough confidence to no longer treat a recipe as gospel. The crust now gets made a full day in advance, and I've experimented with different flours. Most of all, I enjoy the unlikeliness of the recipe's birth—that it took a move to the farmlands of Kentucky for me to learn that my kitchen, once a place of culinary obligation and convenience, could be also be a place of discovery and surprise.

Kentucky Pizza

Adapted from *Bon Appetit*'s 2007 "Pizza Dough" recipe, and their March 1993 "Superfast Vegetarian Pizza" recipe.

Makes a 14-inch pizza, which will feed, with leftovers, two exhausted academics.

Day 1: Making the crust

1 cup bread flour
1 cup wheat flour
1 teaspoon kosher salt
1 teaspoon sugar
1 packet active yeast
¾ cup water
olive oil

If you're using a KitchenAid mixer, put the flours, salt, and sugar in its bowl. Mix them with a whisk so they can all become friendly. Affix the dough hook attachment. If you're using a food processor, put this stuff in bowl and pulse a few times to mix.

Your water needs to be somewhere between 110 and 120 degrees; I can usually achieve this by running my kitchen tap on hot for a bit, filling the measuring cup, and then using a candy thermometer to check the temperature.

Toss in your packet of yeast. Mix it in, and then let it meditate for about 4 minutes. The water should get a foamy beige scum, and you should detect a yeasty aroma emanating from the little science project you've made. If that doesn't happen, you may have gotten some C-yeast, or your water temperature might have been off. Luckily, yeast packets are sold in convenient trios.

Start your processor or mixer. Pour in about half the liquid via the feed tube of the processor, or directly into the bowl of the mixer. Toss in a tablespoon of olive oil. Let the machine run for a minute or two. Add the rest of the liquid and another tablespoon of oil. Let the machine run another minute. You want the dough to arrive at a state of smooth springiness—the best way to confirm this is to stop the machine and give the mass a poke. If the surface feels like it's pushing back against your finger in a friendly way, you're done. If it feels like your finger is just sinking into the surface, and the dough is sullenly ignoring you, give it a little more time in the machine.

Dump your dough into a large, oiled bowl. Shepherd the mass into something ball-like, cover the bowl loosely with plastic wrap, and put it somewhere the cat can't investigate (I put mine on top of the fridge). Leave it until you're ready to make your pizza the next day.

Day 2: The Rest of It

2 tablespoons olive oil
5–7 ounces zucchini, ¼ -inch dice
5–7 ounces yellow squash, ¼ -inch dice

$\longrightarrow$

1–2 teaspoons chopped fresh
   rosemary
½ teaspoon crushed red pepper
2 medium garlic cloves, minced
12 ounce jar of tomato-based pasta
   sauce
¾ cup shredded mozzarella
¾ cup shredded smoked mozzarella
¼–⅓ cup oil-packed, sun-dried
   tomatoes, quickly rinsed to
   remove excess oil, then sliced
cornmeal

Retrieve your bowl of risen dough. Enjoy the smug satisfaction of having remembered to make your dough in advance. Lightly flour a surface, dump the dough onto it, gently knead it a few times so it deflates, then shape it into a ball. Loosely cover with plastic wrap and allow it to rise again for at least 30 minutes.

Preheat your oven to 425.

Heat the oil in a medium-sized skillet over medium heat. Toss in the diced vegetables, then your rosemary and crushed pepper. Sauté until crisp-tender, about 5 minutes (the oven will finish cooking them). Remove the skillet from the heat and set aside.

When your dough has finished its second rise, remove it from the surface. Lay down a roughly squarish sheet of parchment paper. Scatter some cornmeal over it.

Pick up your dough with one hand, and raise your other hand in a fist. Set the dough on your knuckles, and let the dough slump over them. It'll be like your fist is wearing a beret. Place the beret on the cornmeal-covered parchment paper. Poke and stretch the dough out with your fingertips and palms until it's about 14 inches around, and the surface is generally of a uniform thickness. If the dough seems like it's growing tough, cover it with some plastic wrap and wait for a few minutes, so it can relax a bit.

Once the dough is stretched out, cover it with the sauce. Scatter the garlic over the sauce, then scatter the cheeses. Distribute the sun-dried tomatoes evenly over the surface. Scatter zucchini-squash mixture over all that. Putting the cooked vegetables over the tomatoes protects the latter from charring.

Bake for 18 minutes on a pizza stone until the cheese bubbles.

NICKY BEER is the author of *The Octopus Game* (Carnegie Mellon, 2015), winner of the 2016 Colorado Book Award for Poetry, and *The Diminishing House* (Carnegie Mellon, 2010), winner of the 2011 Colorado Book Award for Poetry. She is an assistant professor at the University of Colorado Denver, where she coedits the journal *Copper Nickel*.

SIMON RICH
SIMON'S SARDINE SANDWICH

My grandparents couldn't believe I loved sardines. When they were growing up, canned fish was a last resort, a cheap and desperate way to stretch a paycheck. I come from a long line of sardine-eaters, but I'm the first one in my family to eat the things by choice.

Sardines may be cheap, but they're also pretty decadent. They're full of salt and oil (particularly if you get the kind that's "packed in salt and oil.") And the servings are huge because the tins are packed like, you know, sardines. King Oscar stuffs 12 in every can—an entire school of fish.

When I eat sardines, I like to imagine that they're regular sized fish and that I'm a large monster. Sometimes, if nobody is around, I'll even speak to the sardines in a monster voice. "There's no escape," I'll say, or, "Try and escape." I imagine the sardines straining against the mustard, struggling to swim to freedom. There's fear in their eyes, but also respect. I'm an impressive monster to them and they're proud to have been "beaten by the best."

Here's the recipe my grandparents taught me.

Simon's Sardine Sandwich

1 Thomas' English muffin
1 can King Oscar sardines, packed in salt and oil
1 white onion
mustard

Toast both halves of the muffin. Slather on mustard. Throw on the sardines and some chopped onions. Serve open face. Devour.

SIMON RICH has written comedy for *The New Yorker,* Pixar, and *Saturday Night Live*. He has published two novels and three collections of humor pieces, and his novels and short stories have been translated into over a dozen languages. In 2015, *Man Seeking Woman,* a television comedy series based on Rich's book *The Last Girlfriend on Earth,* premiered on FXX. His latest book is called *Spoiled Brats*.

THE MAIN DISH

FRANCESCA LIA BLOCK
HOW TO FALL IN LOVE

drive to the oracle in the rain
bring white tapers, a pink rose, rose quartz
a miniature white horse
incense, a tiny goddess your father made
a silk pouch
the knight of cups
a crystal phallus

get lost

arrive at the oracle's in tears

"magic responds well when the energy is topsy turvy
i don't know why" she'll say

she will be feline and tall with a soft sway of hips
leading you up the stairs

write a goodbye note to the one who will never leave
his wife
burn it
ignore the way the flames try to reach out for you
later, you will scatter the ashes at a crossroads
where the street lamps have gone out*

tell the oracle, "i'm not ready, i'm a mess"
let her gently suggest you try anyway

why not?
sometimes the magic likes a mess

with the things you have brought
make a charm for your beloved
bless it with the elements
write him a letter
tell him how you see him
and how he sees you
let her summon the spirits,
yours and his
hear her whistle and chant
feel the rain and wind enter the room
feel your mother's ghost caress your face
smile
your hands open on your thighs
think, "this is a lovely way to spend an evening"

meet the oracle's husband in the kitchen
she summoned him this way
he has brought her food and sits on a stool
long-legged and poetic
just who she longed for

drive home
*(this is when to scatter the ashes)

put the charm in your bed
under your pillow
look closely for signs
pay good attention
the man in the cafe reading Melville
who smiles at you—lovely
the wet mark on cement that looks like a heart
the architect with the blue eyes who writes you online

go out with him
have tea and listen, watch
don't worry if he plays it a little cool
surfers do that
your best friend will say
ask her if you should reach out to him
heed her advice
let him pursue you
not as a game
but to allow you both
the great pleasure

meet him at the restaurant
park on the roof
touch his arm
tell him he has an artist's hands
(he does)
ask him what his favorite food is
(apple crumble)
let him walk you to your car
watch as he realizes why you parked there
with a view of the magic hotel and your little town
twinkling below
gone with the wind
and the wizard of oz
were made here

let him kiss you
snuggle against him
see how you fit

go home and write poems
don't send them
not yet.

part 2

in spite of your friends' warnings make dinner for the
architect
salmon with honey mustard sauce
butternut squash soup
that your mother made on holidays
apple crumble
from her handmade cookbook
create a playlist
arcade fire, black keys, silversun
light some candles and wear something made of silk
ask questions, listen to him talk
tell him about you
watch how he reacts
let him kiss you

he will taste of apples, butter, cinnamon
sunshine
whisper poems down his throat
maybe let him sleep
over in your bed
the one you bought when your mother died
only two other men have slept in it with you
make sure this one's worth it

in the morning
maybe he'll go with you
to the memorial
for the woman who played your alter ego in chicago
fifteen years ago
and died of cancer just last month

part 3

wake up from a dream about fighting with your ex
check your email
see one from the man you are dating
see the word "regret"
read that he's cutting it off
whisper over and over to yourself in the dawn "you
are okay, you are okay"
realize that this is bad, this time it's pretty fucking bad
you haven't felt quite like this
since the morning after your mother died

$\longrightarrow$

your belly full of something gelatinous
try to get back to sleep

there's a love charm under your pillow
now it just feels like rocks
email your female tribe
call your brother
call your ex husband
let him tell you that "it's not about you"
though you're pretty sure it is
text the man you were trying to stop loving
when you fell for this new man
when he calls only talk about work
this will protect you both
call your therapist

cry
walk your dog
take a bath
make a kale smoothie
take your vitamins
write a poem
go to work
be glad that you cooked dinner for someone
it's good practice
for when the right one comes along
remember that love love love
it is you
it is you
it is you

Baked Salmon

½ pound wild Alaskan salmon
   half a lemon
1 teaspoon mustard
1 teaspoon honey
salt and pepper, to taste

Rinse the salmon. Combine the other ingredients and put them in a Ziploc bag. Put the salmon in the bag and shake it until coated. Marinate for one hour. Bake at 350 for about half an hour in a glass dish with a touch of olive oil.

Butternut Squash Soup

1 small butternut squash
2 small yams, peeled and cubed
2 carrots, cut
1 onion, cubed
1 tablespoon olive oil
salt and pepper, to taste

Cut the squash in half. Place in a glass pan with a little water and bake at 350 for about 1 hour or until soft

Set aside to cool.

Sauté onion in olive oil until translucent. Add the yams and carrots. Sauté briefly. Add about 5 cups water. Cook until the vegetables are just soft.

Peel and scoop the squash. Add to soup.

Blend in blender. Add salt and pepper to taste.

Apple "Betty"

3 or 4 tart/sweet red apples
¾ cup organic brown sugar
¾ cup organic rolled oats
½ cup organic flour
1 cube butter

Pare and slice the apples. Put in buttered baking dish.

Mix sugar, oats, and flour. Mix in butter with fingers.

Sprinkle crumbly mixture on top of apples.

Bake (covered first 15 minutes) for about half an hour or more at 350.

Serve warm with vanilla almond milk ice cream.

Kale Smoothie

1 handful raw kale, washed
1 banana, peeled and frozen
1 cup frozen pineapple, berries, or
   mango
2 tablespoons flaxseed oil
2 scoops vanilla protein powder

Combine all ingredients. Drink!

FRANCESCA LIA BLOCK is the author of more than 25 books of fiction, non-fiction, short stories, and poetry. She received the Spectrum Award, the Phoenix Award, the ALA Rainbow Award and the 2005 Margaret A. Edwards Lifetime Achievement Award, and has also published stories, poems, essays and interviews in *The Los Angeles Times, The L.A. Review of Books, Spin, Nylon, Black Clock,* and *Rattle* among others. In addition to writing, she teaches fiction workshops at UCLA Extension, Antioch University, and privately in Los Angeles where she was born, raised, and currently still lives with her two children and her dog.

NELSON DEMILLE
ADVERSITY IS THE MOTHER OF INVENTION: G.I. SPAM & BEANS WITH A.1. STEAK SAUCE

I was born during World War II, a time of food rationing, which in retrospect had little effect on the already poor quality of American cuisine. In fact, the food was so bad that less was better. I wasn't old enough to actually remember much of this, though I do recall my mother and her friends talking endlessly about what was available and where to get certain items. I don't mean to give the impression that I went to bed hungry; there was plenty of food available, but not much variety. Incidentally, my ration card, which my mother found and gave to me years later, stated, under

"Occupation," the word "Baby," meaning more milk or something. Lucky me.

Much of the food available during those years seemed to come out of a can (which had to be "recycled" for the war effort, long before it became fashionable to separate your garbage). So, my formative food years were heavily influenced by canned food, including Carnation evaporated milk, which I loathe to this day.

I did, however, develop a taste for canned meat and canned vegetables that has stayed with me long past the

$\longrightarrow$

time when I should have switched to fresh produce. I suppose if we are what we eat, I am a can of Campbell's Pork and Beans, and a tin of Spam.

My college years, living in an apartment, reinforced not only my taste for canned food and processed meat—such as Dinty Moore's Beef Stew in a big round tin—but also my belief that one should let others do the cooking, and I would do the heating, if necessary. I think of Chef Boyardee's ravioli simmering in its own can on the stove as I write this. (The meat raviolis are better than the cheese, which tends to fall apart.)

Then I spent three years in the Army, where a lot of the mess hall food also came out of cans. Very large cans, with no brand names, though the essence of the industrial recipes came through. I mean, this stuff was tested for years and the ingredients were blended and pre-cooked to perfection.

I did have some issues with the C-rations that I ate for a year in Vietnam. They came in olive drab cans and mostly were dated 1943—ironically, the year of my birth. But, adversity is the mother of invention, and the troops soon learned how to make C-rations edible with a few dashes of Tabasco sauce (available at the PX) or even homemade soy sauce that we bought from local villagers. Interestingly, the Vietnamese would not trade anything for our C-rations, so we had to pay cash for the soy sauce, or for something called nuoc mam, which we discovered was fermented fish parts. Bad as that sounds, it did perk up the 25-year-old canned meat and veggies. American ingenuity.

The C-rats, as we called them, were heated directly in the can by putting something called a heat tab under them. One lit heat tab, about the size of an alka-seltzer tablet, could heat an eight-ounce can of, say, pork and lima beans, or beef and potatoes. A half tablet would heat a four-ounce can of reconstituted eggs. But, as we discovered, to heat is to release flavors that may best be left in a dormant state.

Every now and then the mess sergeant would send out to the troops what are called K-rations. These are not individual C-ration cans, but bigger cans of food that are meant to be shared. One day, the resupply helicopter delivered quart-sized cans of cooked beans of recent vintage that tasted very much like stateside Campbell's Pork and Beans. We hit the jackpot. Also in our resupply were quart-sized cans of Spam.

One of the guys in my platoon was a whiz with C-rats and K-rats, and he immediately knew what to do. First we cut the Spam into one-inch cubes. Next, we borrowed a rice kettle from the locals, and mixed the beans and the cubed Spam, then placed the kettle over a wood fire. Finally, one guy had a bottle of stateside A.1. Steak Sauce in his backpack, and he poured it into the bubbling cauldron. Voila! The aroma itself made 40 mouths water. Even a few rice farmers came around to see what was cooking.

I can still remember the taste and smell of this meal, almost 40 years later. Of course, everything tastes better when it's cooked outdoors, and when your stomach is growling, but even today when I make this at home I am carried back to that moment.

Over time, I have tweaked this recipe, and I now add powdered mustard to the pot. Sometimes even a dash of Tabasco. But that's it. Don't try to get creative.

Another caveat: Spam now comes in various flavors, such as teriyaki, jalapeño, and hickory smoke. Do not use these. Spam also comes with cheese, or black pepper, and even with Tabasco sauce already added. These are all good as a main meat course, but not as an ingredient in this dish. And finally, Spam is also offered with less fat and less salt. I don't need to say the obvious, but what's the point of low fat, low salt Spam, right?

So, use only the original Spam. And do not overcook, since it is already cooked, and just needs heating. But you can let the Spam, beans, and A.1. sauce marinate for an hour or so before you apply heat. Also, I prefer Campbell's Pork and Beans, but Van Camp's are good, too. It's all the same stuff. It's just the Spam and A.1. Steak Sauce that cannot be substituted.

G.I. Spam & Beans

2 cans pork and beans
1 can original SPAM, cubed
A.1. Steak Sauce to taste
a pinch mustard powder, and/or a
    dash Tabasco (optional)
salt to taste

Pour the beans into a pot, add cubed Spam and A.1. Steak Sauce, stir, and let it marinate for 30–60 minutes. Then, heat until it's warm, and add mustard powder and/or Tabasco. Stir. Serve warm in a bowl and eat with a soup spoon.

If you're making this for your family, you may find yourself dining alone—and probably sleeping alone. But just eat up, and thank God you're an American.

NELSON DEMILLE is the bestselling author of: *By the Rivers of Babylon, Cathedral, The Talbot Odyssey, Word of Honor, The Charm School, The Gold Coast, The General's Daughter, Spencerville, Plum Island, Mayday, The Lion's Game, Up Country, Night Fall, Wild Fire, The Gate House, The Lion, The Panther, The Quest,* and *Radiant Angel.* He was a First Lieutenant in the United States Army (1966-69), and saw action as an infantry platoon leader with the First Cavalry Division in Vietnam. He was decorated with the Air Medal, Bronze Star, and the Vietnamese Cross of Gallantry. He has three children, Lauren, Alexander, and James, and lives on Long Island with his wife, Sandy.

ANN HOOD
SPAGHETTI CARBONARA

In the Italian-American household where I grew up, red sauce ruled. Every Monday, my grandmother Mama Rose made gallons of it in a giant tarnished pot. She started the sauce by cooking sausage in oil, then frying onions in that same oil and adding various forms of canned tomatoes: crushed, puréed, paste. Without measuring, she'd toss in the ingredients. Red wine. Sugar. Salt and pepper. Parsley from her garden. The sauce simmered until, as Mama Rose used to say, it wasn't bitter.

On Mondays, my after school snack was always that freshly made sauce on slabs of bread, a taste sensation that I have never been able to duplicate. For the rest of the week, red sauce topped chicken, veal, pasta, meatballs, and even fried eggs for something called Eggs in Purgatory, which we ate on Friday nights when we Catholics could not eat meat. We ate our pasta and all of our parmigianas, from chicken to eggplant, drenched in

sauce. There was always a gravy dish of extra sauce on the table, and we all used it liberally.

I led a fairly protected life in my small hometown in Rhode Island, surrounded by other southern Italian immigrants. And until I was out of college and working as an international flight attendant for TWA, Italian sauce was always red. Suddenly, at the age of 21, I found myself in a Ralph Lauren uniform flying all over the world feeding passengers on 747s. I was often struck by homesickness during those early days of flying, so the first time I had a layover in Italy, I ordered spaghetti carbonara. Perhaps on that afternoon in Rome, I believed spaghetti would span the miles between me and my family, connect us in some way. Instead, what the officious waiter in the bow tie put in front of me, was yellow. And speckled with brown.

"Uh," I managed, "I ordered the spaghetti carbonara?"

What followed was a rush of dramatic Italian, much pointing to the menu and the spaghetti, and then the waiter's departure, in a huff.

I was hungry and alone in Rome, the rest of the crew asleep or off shopping for cheap designer handbags. What could I do, but eat?

I took my first tentative bite: salty with cheese and bacon, creamy with eggs, the spaghetti perfectly al dente. It may have been the most delicious thing I had ever eaten. I tried to thank the waiter, to explain my folly in trying to send it back, but he ignored me. But, it didn't matter; I left that restaurant intoxicated by spaghetti carbonara.

In those days, I was not much of a cook, but I knew I needed to learn to make that dish. For the first time in my life, I scoured cookbooks and tried different versions. Back then, Italian cookbooks were few, and for some reason I could only find terrible recipes. Recipes that used cream, or added mushrooms or onions. None of them were even close to my blissful dish.

Then one day in a bookstore in Boston I found an old cookbook filled with the recipes of Rome. I read the one for spaghetti carbonara; it was devoid of anything except bacon, eggs and cheese. I bought the book, and the ingredients, and made it that very night.

I never really expected to duplicate the experience of that meal in Rome. But that night, I came close. And I used that recipe for every dinner party I had over the next couple of decades. Or, I should say, some version of it, because over time I lost that cookbook, which didn't really matter because by then I'd tweaked the recipe enough, increasing the bacon, decreasing the cheese, changing proportions each time.

While I still love my red sauce roots, spaghetti carbonara has become my comfort food. I make it for myself when I'm feeling lonely, and I make it to welcome others into my home.

Spaghetti Carbonara

1 pound spaghetti
a little extra virgin olive oil
1 pound either slab bacon or
   pancetta, diced
3 eggs, beaten
2 egg yolks, set aside
lots of good freshly grated
   Parmesan cheese
black pepper
scallions, chopped

Start the water boiling to cook the spaghetti. Make sure to throw a good amount of salt into the water.

While that's going on, coat the bottom of a skillet with extra virgin olive oil and heat it enough so that when you throw in the bacon (or pancetta) it immediately starts to sizzle.

Cook the bacon until it's good and crispy, then turn off the heat and leave it in the pan. DO NOT DRAIN!

When the spaghetti is al dente, drain it and throw it in the skillet with the cooked bacon, reserving about a quarter cup of the water it was cooked in.

Add the beaten eggs to the skillet and start to toss it all together. The heat of the spaghetti will melt the eggs and everything should start to get nice and creamy. Add that ¼ cup of cooking water as you toss. This helps with the creaminess factor.

Put the spaghetti, now combined with the eggs and bacon, into a pretty serving bowl and begin to toss with the cheese. I add it in ¼–½ cup amounts, tossing each time. Your goal here is to nicely coat all the spaghetti with cheese.

Drop those two egg yolks you reserved onto the top and toss them in too, which usually leads to adding another ¼ cup of cheese.

Grind coarse black pepper on top, and don't be stingy with it.

Garnish with a little bit of chopped scallions. (This is optional, but a nice touch.)

ANN HOOD is the author of the bestselling novels *The Knitting Circle, The Red Thread,* and *Somewhere off the Coast of Maine.* Her latest novel, *The Obituary Writer,* was named one of the Best Books Of 2013 by Amazon. Her memoir, *Comfort,* was named one of the best non-fiction books of 2008 by *Entertainment Weekly* and was a NYT Editors' Choice.

GIDEON BOK
BLACK TRUMPETS

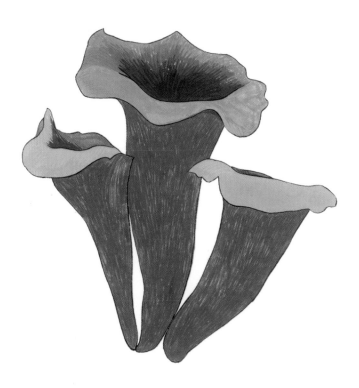

Sometime in late summer, go out and look in gently sloping areas of the forest, especially in places where water flows in the wet season and then eventually drains away. They are hard to spot at first because they look like dead leaves, but once you find them, you'll suddenly be able to find them again and again, especially after you discover how obscenely delicious they are.

Up close, black trumpets look like velvety black or grey cones poking out from dead leaves under broad leafed trees such as beech and oak. They are hollow, and, unlike some mushrooms, they do not have a separation between the stalk and the cap. In fact, they don't have a cap at all, but are more like a cone made of thick paper or rubber that is curled over at the top. With their horn-like shape, they've been called *the trumpets of the dead,* as if they're in fact horns blown by dead people

buried underground. Don't let that dark image dissuade you; this is just an attempt to keep the competition from taking all the mushrooms.

Of course, you *could* just buy them in a fancy store, where they'll be expensive but possibly still good. But, they're infinitely better if you get them yourself in the woods on a beautiful late summer's day with fun people. If you find some you will probably find a LOT, and there are often chanterelles nearby, too. (Those are easier to spot but not as delicious.) If you get some chanterelles, throw them in, too, but the best-case scenario would be lots of black trumpets.

When you pick black trumpets, pinch off the bottom of the stem. This will leave almost all of the soil in the woods where it belongs, as opposed to in your pasta, where it does not.

Black Trumpet Ravioli

black trumpet mushrooms
ricotta cheese
Parmigiano-Reggiano
unbleached all-purpose flour
overgrown garlic scapes
rosemary
very fresh eggs
lots of butter
salt and pepper
ideally served with a good wine, but
    beer works, too

This dish is best if you live in the country, preferably with a garden, chickens, forest, a picnic table, and amazing friends who visit in late summer and are happy to spend an afternoon gathering black trumpets with you.

When you have gathered enough, bring your friends home, split and cut them up, and throw away the slimy parts (of the mushrooms, I mean). With your finger, separate the stem of the mushroom and evict any earwigs and/or dirt, then chop them into little bits. Melt some butter in a pan and throw the mushroom bits into the butter. Gently simmer, and take care not to burn the butter.

After the mushrooms have simmered for 10 minutes or so, remove them from the heat and combine them with some ricotta cheese, salt and pepper, and a healthy amount of grated Parmesan cheese. The ricotta can be any old ricotta, but the Parmesan has to be good quality, i.e. genuine Parmigiano-Reggiano. This is important. If you balk at the price, think about how much you saved by foraging your own black trumpets. *Do not skimp on the Parmesan*. Keep tasting the mix to be sure the amount of salt and pepper is good. The mixture should be slightly pasty, but not too dry.

Next, make the pasta dough. (You can actually begin this earlier, since it will need to sit awhile. Better yet, have one of your friends begin the dough while you tend to the

mushrooms). I use 1 cup all-purpose unbleached flour and 1 large (very fresh) egg per person, but I eat a lot. Put the flour in a bowl with a well in the center, add the beaten egg in the well, and mix together with a fork and then begin kneading. The pasta dough should be more dry than wet, with just enough moisture to bring the flour together. If you must, add a tiny bit of water. Knead the dough for 10–15 minutes, until it is smooth and elastic. Then, wrap it in plastic and let it relax for 45 minutes.

Dust the tabletop with flour, and then roll the dough out in thin sheets (unless you have a pasta maker, in which case, use the second-to-thinnest setting). Then, get a small glass that's bigger than a shot glass, but smaller than a pint glass. Press the glass into the dough to make a bunch of circles, and then place the circles on a (well dusted) plate or sheet of wax paper. Then put a small dollop of the mushroom/cheese mixture in the middle of the circle. You can wet the edge of the circle with some beaten egg or water. (Egg works best, but I've found that water will do.) Then—careful not to have any of the filling too close to any of the edges—place another circle of pasta dough on top, and crimp the edges, so that there is a seal. Try to get as much air out of the pouch as you can, but don't go crazy.

If you have garlic scapes that have been allowed to grow to the point where the little tiny bulbs in the top of the scape have formed into little balls, called bulbils, separate those out, and

remove the skin (very important) on the outside of the little balls. Do this by rubbing them between your hands.

Melt a few sticks of butter in a pan, and throw the little garlic bulbils in. If you don't have garlic scapes you can squeeze in a little bit of garlic, but not too much. One clove or even a bit less is plenty, since too much garlic will overpower the trumpets and that is not forgivable.

Let the butter simmer awhile with the bulbils, and add salt and pepper to taste.

Then, grab a sprig of fresh rosemary and throw it in the butter. This is the pièce de résistance of the dish, which was a moment of genius from Jena, who is one of our very special people. What it does with the flavor of the trumpets is kind of sublime.

Boil a big pot of water and place the ravioli in, turning the heat down so the water's not boiling rapidly with the ravioli in there. They don't need very long, maybe 2 minutes, to cook the pasta and to heat the inside a bit. If you weren't diligent with crimping, or the filling was too close to the edge of the ravioli, this is the moment of reckoning.

If possible, scoop out the ravioli with one of those big strainer spoons. If not, drain very carefully, as ravioli don't respond well to violence.

As quickly as you can, plate the ravioli, spoon the butter/bulbil mixture on them, grate some Parmesan on top, and freak out.

GIDEON BOK is a professor of Painting at Boston University. He earned a B.A. from Hampshire College and a M.F.A. from Yale University. He has been awarded a John Simon Guggenheim Memorial Fellowship as well as the Hassam, Speicher, Betts, and Symons Fund Purchase Award through the American Academy of Arts and Letters. Commentary on Bok's work has appeared in *The New York Times, The Boston Globe, ARTnews,* and *Time Out New York.* He is represented by Alpha Gallery in Boston and Steven Harvey Fine Art in NYC.

RUTH REICHL
BLACK BEANS WITH ROSITA

"I have an idea…"

Whenever my mother said that, the rest of us cringed. Mom was always up for an adventure—especially if the adventurer was one of us.

We'd just reached the top of the pyramid at Chichen Itza, having walked up all 91 steps, when Mom uttered the fateful sentence. I hoped the idea did not involve more climbing; the sun was blazing hot, and down below, the Yucatan spread beneath us. I peered down, trying to find our hotel, wondering how long it would be before we could go back and go swimming.

But Mom wasn't looking down; she was looking at our guide, Juan, with a worrisome glint in her eyes. "Didn't you say your daughter was the same age as Ruthie?"

"Si," he said, "Rosita is eight years old."

"I thought so!" Mom looked triumphant. "What would you think about having Ruthie stay with you while we go on to Guatemala?"

I looked at Dad, to see if he was in on this crazy idea, but he seemed as surprised as I was. He put out his hand, as if to stop Mom. "Don't you think we should discuss this?"

"What is there to discuss?" Mom was breezy. "It's a wonderful opportunity for Ruthie to learn how other people live. It's only a week, but children pick up languages so quickly that she'll probably be fluent in Spanish by the time we pick her up."

The next thing I knew we were in the marketplace, buying a hammock for me to hang up beside Rosita's, along with a plate, a knife, and a fork. I remember the plate, one of those aluminum numbers divided into three sections like a tv dinner tray. It was bright magenta.

The first night I lay swinging in my hammock, tears running silently down my face, terrified. Outside the small casita the murmur of Spanish filled my ears, incomprehensible sounds. What was I doing there? But I was used to my mother's quirks—it was just one of the many interesting experiences she dreamed up—and Rosita was thrilled to have a temporary sister. I wonder if my mother paid her parents? In any case, they were very kind, and by the time my own family reappeared I was almost sorry to see them.

Sadly, I had not become fluent in Spanish, although I had learned two things. One was Rosita's favorite jump rope refrain: *"Buenas dias, no hay tortillas. Buenas noches, no hay frijoles."* The other was how to make those frijoles; a big pot of beans was always sitting on her mother's stove, and we'd run in and out of the kitchen, scooping warm beans onto tortillas whenever hunger hit.

Yucatan Black Beans

epazote
2 cups dry black beans
2 chopped onions
1 chili (optional)
4 tablespoons duck fat (or whatever kind of animal fat you have leftover from cooking)
salt to taste
unsweetened chocolate, grated (optional)

There are two essential elements here. The first is epazote, an herb that grows wild all over the Yucatan (and also in Manhattan's Central Park). It has a musky, faintly oregano-like flavor, and is supposed to have a carminative effect; nobody around Merida ever made a pot of beans without throwing in a few sprigs. And the second is a healthy amount of lard; in Merida black beans were not a vegetarian delight.

Wash 2 cups of dry black beans and pick through them, discarding stones and broken beans. Put them in a pot (preferably a ceramic one), cover them with a few inches of water and leave them to soak overnight.

In the morning drain the water. Put the beans back in the pot with 6 cups of water and a few sprigs of epazote. Add a couple of chopped onions, a chili if you feel like it, and about 4 tablespoons of whatever kind of animal fat you have leftover from cooking. Pork or bacon fat is wonderful; duck fat is even better. Bring it to a boil, turn the heat down, cover loosely and let it burble happily to itself until the beans are soft. This can take anywhere from an hour to three, depend on the age of your beans. (Beans that have been sitting around gathering dust for a while will be more reluctant to relax.)

When they're done, add salt to taste. Rosita's mother sometimes grated a little unsweetened chocolate in as well, and I've been known to add a bit of soy sauce or cream sherry.

These are great sprinkled with queso fresco and wrapped in warm corn tortillas.

RUTH REICHL is the author of four memoirs, a novel, and two cookbooks. She is the former restaurant critic of *The Los Angeles Times* and *The New York Times,* and former Editor in Chief of *Gourmet* magazine.

SWOON
RATATOUILLE ON THE MISSISSIPPI

It's Arielle's and my turn to cook lunch for the crew of the Miss Rockaway Armada. Lucky for me; cooking while the Mississippi River goes by is a supreme pleasure, and Arielle is a ridiculously good chef. She wants to make ratatouille.

There are six rafts in total, bound together in a line, 110 feet long; the galley is the middle raft. Thirty-three of my friends and I built the Miss Rockaway Armada entirely out of garbage: scrap metal, donated screws, wood dumpstered or begged from construction sites, styrofoam for pontoons. Together we've created a fantastical floating home, and together we're navigating the stretch of the Mississippi River from Minneapolis to St. Louis over the course of two summers, sailing approximately 800 miles.

On this particular day, we have a choice to make: cross Pool 13—the widest stretch of the Mississippi, limestone cliffs on either side—or wait. It's an unusually windy day; locals have advised us to wait. We decide to cross. We're almost out of potable water, and the weather is closing in on us. Maybe we can clear it before the multi-day storm sets in?

As Arielle and I put the finishing touches on the ratatouille, I reach for my water glass at the exact moment that it goes flying across the counter. Within seconds, we're hit with four to five foot swells. Suddenly, the rafts are smashing against themselves, threatening to rip our hand-hewn home to shreds. Everyone on board is in hysterics.

We somehow manage to pull the skiff around into towing position to try to give us extra power, but it unexpectedly runs out of gas. I watch helplessly as Hanna tries to funnel fuel into a boat that's going nearly vertical every 30 seconds or so. Then the ropes attaching the back three rafts break loose on one side, causing them to careen around, repeatedly bashing into the front rafts. All of the crew is on these front rafts, barely hanging on to various masts and doorways.

George volunteers to cut the remaining ropes on the back rafts. This entails sliding himself out over a thin piece of piping next to the desperately churning propeller, while Erica holds onto him by the back of his pants as he saws through the ropes with a steak knife.

Free of the back three rafts we are lighter, faster. We motor on, and somehow, slowly, then all at once, we find we have reached the calm shallows near shore.

We pull over and tie off to a tree. Robinson begins splinting a broken finger; some people are crying, some stand in stunned silence, some are already laughing it off. Looking around for something to do, some way to make people feel better, I see that our huge simmering pot of ratatouille and couscous that went flying off the stove had managed to lodge itself under the galley benches, completely intact. It's even still warm.

So Arielle and I scrounge up what bowls and spoons we can find, and we serve up the most delicious steaming bowls of ratatouille that any group of stunned scallywags was ever grateful to eat.

Ratatouille for 30–35 people

½ cup extra virgin olive oil (we bought ours in bulk from the co-op 3 towns north)
8 cloves garlic
3 onions
4 bell peppers
15 tomatoes (these were delivered from the gardens of people who came to see us on the river)
4 large eggplants
10 zucchini (also from the gardens)

tons of basil (god, I'll never forget those gardens)
cumin
a bit of thyme
a few pinches cayenne
black pepper
and as salty as you like it
plus 12 cups couscous, cooked until tender

Start with the garlic and olive oil in a huge cooking pot. Add onions and peppers and let them brown a little. Add the tomatoes and cover the pot, letting the juices begin to release and simmer. Then, add the eggplant and zucchini and spices. Cover and simmer, stirring occasionally for the next 30 minutes or so. When the concoction becomes aromatic, tender, and stewy, without overcooking the zucchini and eggplant, you're ready—either to eat, or to finally face the storm.

SWOON (b. Caledonia Curry) is an artist working in drawing, printmaking, site specific installations, street interventions, and community-based projects. From 2006 to 2009, she constructed and navigated a flotilla of sculptural rafts made from recycled materials down the Mississippi and Hudson rivers, and across the Adriatic Sea to Venice. In 2010 she cofounded Konbit Shelter and built a community center and two homes in earthquake-devastated Haiti, integrating her creative process into a sustainable reconstruction effort. Recently, Swoon founded a non-profit, known as The Heliotrope Foundation, to support her community based-endeavors.

SONYA CLARK
PERFUME AND PEPPER

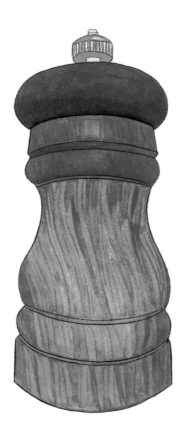

I don't know when the shift occurred. She used to ask me, "How are you?" Some years ago, I realized instead she had developed the habit of asking, "Where are you?" As if the location of my body indicated something of my mental, physical, emotional condition. It must have happened gradually in direct correlation to my growing appetite (really, my need) for travel. Her "how" morphed into "where."

Born and raised in Jamaica, my mother left her home country at 28, following my father, who had immigrated to Washington, DC many years before she arrived. Theirs was a decade of long-distance courting in the days of thin, onion skin, airmail letters that took weeks to arrive. That was her normal: love and distance. Despite all that, she seems tickled by my peripatetic

inclinations. It's a kind of maternal pride, I suspect— she raised a woman curious enough to travel the world with or without company.

But as a first generation American, I need different vantage points to understand the place in which I was born, so off I go: Ethiopia, Italy, India, South Africa, Morocco, Indonesia, or Australia. When we chat on the phone, if I am anywhere but home, she says, "I never rubbed pepper on your feet as a child. I don't know how you travel so." It's a common Caribbean sentiment—like a rolling stone that gathers no moss, hot feet don't stay in one place.

There were family vacations with my dad and sister, but Mom and I traveled alone together only once. That trip to coastal Maine lives in our memory as something almost mythical; spruce trees sprouted from glacially transported boulders, the air spiced with evergreen and brine. We had hoped for more trips like that but now travel is hard on her aging body and I sense an increasingly vicarious desire in her question: "Where are you?"

The thing is my mother is with me wherever I go. She's a naturally beautiful woman who never wears perfume or any trace of makeup. Yet, when the air catches any combination of ginger, thyme, garlic, allspice, and onion, no matter where I am in the world, she is by my side. These are the spices in the first recipe she ever taught me to cook, rice and peas. A bit of her homeland that she translated to me: Coconut milk, yes. Rice, yes. Gungo peas, yes. And the scent of her, imbued with those seasonings, yes. Her fragrance is with me and my peppery feet always.

Jamaican Rice and Peas

coconut milk (13.5 ounce can)
½ teaspoon allspice (whole seeds)
¼ cup diced onion or 2–3 diced scallions
1 clove garlic, chopped
¼ teaspoon fresh grated ginger
2–3 sprigs fresh thyme
gungo peas (also known as pigeon peas or gandules, 15-ounce can)
2 cups long grain white basmati rice
pinch of salt

Add coconut milk to a pot and simmer with allspice, ginger, garlic, thyme, scallions/or sautéed onions. Cover and simmer for 5 minutes. Stir in can of undrained gungo peas, rice, salt, and a coconut milk can's worth of water (about 1 ¾ cups). Cover loosely with lid and let cook 15–20 minutes over low heat until tender. Fluff with a fork. Remove thyme stems and serve.

SONYA CLARK is professor and chair of the Craft and Material Studies department in the School of the Arts at Virginia Commonwealth University. She is known for making works from hair, cloth, and combs to address race and cultural identity. Her work has been exhibited in over 300 museums and galleries in Europe, Africa, Asia, Australia, and the Americas. Sonya lives in Richmond with her husband, Darryl Harper, a jazz musician and chair of the Music department at VCU.

LAUREL NAKADATE AND RICK MOODY
DINNER WITH LAUREL & RICK

Laurel and I can't cook worth a shit, and we rarely spend more than ten minutes in the kitchen, and personally I think that eating is something that you do to avoid starvation, rather than something which should be done out of sybaritic delight or aesthetic bliss.

That said, I do make a really good vegetarian carrot and parsnip soup. It is humble but appealing. I made it for Laurel, also a vegetarian, the first time she came to my house to visit.

One night, as I prepared the soup, Laurel made pizza boats. (On nights of abandon when she was young, she used to make these with her father and two brothers. They were considered the high point of the week.) I was really skeptical and thought that she was about to feed me a pretend food, a simulated recipe, perhaps because she was trying to get rid of some stale Italian bread or an old jar of sauce. But, actually, these pizza boats were, and are, the genuine article. Now we feel that the two dishes belong together.

Carrot and Parsnip Soup

carrots (actual carrots, not the fake
    baby carrots)
parsnips
1 white onion
32 ounces of vegetable stock (or
    make your own if you want to do
    it the hard way)
some sour cream
a splash of olive oil

First, slice up the onion and sauté it in olive oil in a big soup pot. Keep sautéing the onions until they get a little bit translucent. (But don't burn them. They just cause problems later if they burn.)

Slice up a bunch of carrots and a bunch of parsnips. The big challenge with this soup is to try to avoid overwhelming the parsnip taste with the carrot taste. Of the two vegetables, the parsnip is the more glorious, and if you do exactly 50-50, the carrot will win the battle of taste. A couple of cups of each is sufficient, but you want a little more parsnip than carrot. Dice them up, but you don't have to be all anal-compulsive about it, because you're going to boil the fuck out of these vegetables and then put them in a food processor.

Once you have the root vegetables diced up, pour the vegetable stock into your pot, and warm it up to the edge of boiling, then toss in the root vegetables. Simmer the whole thing for somewhere around half an hour, or until the vegetables are really soft.

Periodically, Laurel and I disagree about whether it's worth adding *other vegetables* to this soup. I have made it so many times (because I am vegetarian and I like root vegetables a lot) that I get bored of it sometimes, and for this reason I have added turnips (on occasion), though I can't wholeheartedly recommend this, and apples (because I know a good recipe for apple and parsnip purée), which I liked a lot, but which Laurel found too sweet. I think potatoes would probably work perfectly well too, though it's sort of a different taste. Some heirloom carrots would probably be good. Or a rutabaga. It's up to you, really.

After the vegetables are well boiled, you want to get down your food processor, if you have one (I have done it with a blender, too, though that was a bit messy), and purée the whole thing. It'll probably be in two batches, if you have the normal-sized food processor. It'll turn a lovely orange color, and it should be somewhat thick.

You will definitely want some salt. Pepper helps too. Think of the lowly carrot, how it requires a bit of something in order to make its argument boldly.

This is also where the sour cream comes into it. I have used plain yogurt, and that's okay, but you really want the sour cream. It gives the whole thing a savory *identity* somehow. I add about a tablespoon per bowl. You can stir it in yourself.

Pizza Boats

1 baguette of Italian bread
Newman's Own Sockarooni
    Marinara Sauce
shredded mozzarella cheese
toothpicks with flags (any kind of
    flags. You can even personalize
    them for each diner)

Pre-heat the oven to 425.

Slice baguette down the middle lengthwise and then in turn slice the halves horizontally into four pieces. At the end of this procedure, the result will look like six-inch boats. Put the boats on an oven pan.

Spoon the marinara sauce on the bread, and spread it around.

Strew the shredded cheese about the individual "boats." The cheese should be *inside* the perimeter of the boats, because if it spills out, it's going to burn in the oven.

Cook the pizza boats on the oven pan until the mozzarella is fully melted, probably 10–15 minutes depending on your oven. Optional: turn the oven up to 450 for the final 5 minutes, to fully brown the bread. Be sure to keep an eye on the boats. Everybody's oven is different.

While the boats are cooking, you have your chance to create the flags. Cut little pennant-shaped flags out of paper, and draw whatever you want on them. Pierce the toothpicks through the flags so that the flags sort of thread onto the toothpick. If you are a parent who frequently has the kids around while trying to cook, you can enlist the kids to draw on paper and make the little flags while you deal with the pizza boats. That will keep them busy for at least 15 minutes.

After you take the pizza boats out of the oven, stick the flags onto the bow of each boat and serve hot. It's true: the top of your mouth will get burned when you eat these. But that's just part of the experience.

RICK MOODY is the author of six novels, the most recent of which is *Hotels of North America,* as well as three collections of stories, a memoir, and a volume of essays on music. He also sings in The Unspeakable Practices. For LitHub, he writes a monthly column entitled "Rick Moody, Life Coach."

LAUREL NAKADATE is a photographer, filmmaker, performance, and video artist. Her work is in many collections including the Whitney Museum of American Art and the Museum of Modern Art.

JEFFERY RENARD ALLEN
NYAMA CHOMA

I first ate nyama choma in Nairobi in the summer of 2006, during my very first trip to the African continent. A friend took me took a popular restaurant called Carnivore—the name says it all—and it was truly the best thing I had ever tasted (suckling pig and bunny chow are close seconds). Since then, I have enjoyed the dish more times than I can count in Tanzania, my wife's homeland. In Kiswahili, the phrase *nyama choma* literally means "roasted meat," but everyone knows that the meat in question is goat. The meat-loving Masai have been eating nyama choma for centuries, long before someone came up with a name for it in Kiswahili.

(East African joke:

Waiter: What would you like to eat?

Masai man: Meat.

Waiter: And would you like something to drink with that?

Masai man: Yes. Meat.)

In Tanzania, a trip to a nyama choma restaurant is like going to a five-star restaurant in America or Europe; it's a treat, as well as a sign of privilege and prestige. For that reason, Tanzanians usually reserve the dish for special outings with family, friends, or colleagues, or for wedding receptions.

If you don't live in Tanzania or Kenya, your first challenge will be finding good goat meat. In Nairobi or Dar es Salaam, the goat is always served fresh, meaning that it was killed the very same day that you eat it. So fresh goat is the rub. Otherwise it's an easy dish to prepare.

Nyama Choma (Roasted Goat)

2 pounds goat ribs
salt to taste
sliced onions and tomatoes

One kilo (2 pounds) is enough meat for 2 people. As for what cut of the goat to choose, I have found that the ribs are the tastiest part.

Salt the meat. That's it. No marinating, no fancy spices or sauces—none of that. The charm of nyama choma is the fresh meat taste. Put the meat on the grill to roast over a charcoal fire. Keep the flame low so that the ribs cook slowly. It will take a full hour for the meat to roast.

In Kenya, people typically kill the hour by drinking beer and talking. In Tanzania they usually eat small plates of fried food such as chipsi mayai, two eggs fried over easy with strips of white potatoes (french fries). Or they simply eat a plate of chips with salt and ketchup (called "tomato sauce" in Tanzania) or a plate of fried yellow plantains.

Once the hour is up and the meat is done cooking, chop the ribs into small chunks (tips). If you don't have a machete, use a sharp knife. The meat is always served with a simple salad of sliced onions and tomatoes. You may also add a side dish of mchicha, spinach boiled with a bit of tomato, onion, salt, and olive oil. You can even prepare some ugali, dough made from maize flour, a staple that most Tanzanians eat at least once a day, usually in the afternoon since it is filling. A true ugali eater knows how to shape a portion of the dough into a small ball before wrapping it around a piece of goat or spinach. If you are a big eater, nyama choma also goes well with coucou (roasted chicken) or a whole fish like changu (snapper), so feel free to add a plate of either or both. The roasted meat is tasty but tough, so you will need to wash it down with a pint of beer or a bottle or two of soda, such as my favorite, Stoney Tanagawizi, a mild ginger beer from South Africa.

Meal done, lean back in your chair for a while feeling fat and satisfied, with a toothpick between your teeth.

A warning: if you eat your meal in the Tanzanian manner, you will have to ward off bothersome flies. Nyama choma places in Tanzania are not swanky establishments like the Carnivore in Nairobi where measures are taken to keep flies away from the food. (In Nairobi, the plastic table clothes are wiped down with kerosene.) People simply sit outside in cheap plastic chairs around cheap plastic tables and casually wave and brush the flies away. If you are clever, you will figure out exactly where to place your already-gnawed goat bones on the table so that the flies will leave you alone, allowing everyone to feast.

JEFFERY RENARD ALLEN is the author of five books, most recently the novel *Song of the Shank*, which is loosely based on the life of Blind Tom, a 19th-century African-American piano virtuoso and composer who was the first African-American to perform at The White House. The novel won the Firecracker Award and was a finalist for the PEN/Faulkner Award and the IMPAC award. Allen's many other accolades include a Whiting Writers' Award, a grant in Innovative Literature from Creative Capital, a Guggenheim Fellowship, and a Bellagio Fellowship. He is a Professor of Creative Writing at the University of Virginia.

ESMERALDA SANTIAGO
LECHÓN EN VARITA

We were Puerto Rican campesinos, Mami, Papi, seven children. We had a couple of hens that picked at the ground for worms, ants, and grasshoppers. From time to time, a rooster strutted over from doña Ana's yard, chased one of the hens, flapping his wings over her. Then we had eggs, and, if we didn't eat them all, eventually we had chicken for dinner. We had a pig that rolled around a muddy pen in the backyard, eating scraps, taro and batata peels, mango and avocado pits, eggshells; for a while, we had a couple of ducks and rabbits. We even had a goat that ate everything, including the rope around his neck.

Mami and Papi struggled to feed us and we learned not to be squeamish about what was placed before us. We begged for the chicken wings, the neck, the gizzards. We argued over who'd get the roasted pig's crispy tail or ears. We ate tripe stew and salted pig's feet with garbanzos. And all of us understood that our animals were prospective meals. Someday the chickens would be featured in an arroz con pollo. The pig, impaled on a stick over an open fire became the Christmas lechón, while the goat made a warm and saucy cabrito en

fricasé. Everybody wanted the lucky rabbit paws when Mami made fricasé de conejo.

A whole new world of food was introduced to me when we moved to the United States when I was a teenager. Hamburgers, hot dogs, salami, bologna, corned beef and pastrami—I tried it all. But when I left home and could control my own diet, I became a vegetarian. Packaged, sterile meats never tasted right. They were too tender, almost slimy to my tongue, and their bland, processed flavors, unimproved by generous amounts of familiar spices, were insipid compared to the gamy tang I was used to.

When I married Frank, he never complained about the mounds of brown rice that I served with a side of beans seasoned with sofrito, and vegetables sautéed in mojo de ajo or dressed with ajilimojili. Still, I suspected that he ate meat when traveling for work. I didn't miss it when I was at home, but during our frequent trips to Puerto Rico, I couldn't resist the fragrant roadside stands with lechón en varita, escabeche de pulpo, and pavochón. My palate restored to the flavors and textures I remembered, by the time our children entered elementary school we were eating meat liberally seasoned with my homemade adobos.

Then Lucas and Ila wanted a dog.

"A dog needs a lot of time, space, and attention," I said. "The upkeep is expensive and after all that, we can't even eat it."

"That's gross, Mom!"

At that moment I understood just how foreign my childhood had been from the one they were living. I'd grown up in the interior of a Caribbean island, in a rural barrio with no running water or electricity; I'd never owned animals that weren't edible. Culture, economics, and morality intersected in unexpected ways when I remembered myself, barefoot and knobby kneed, happily chasing a scrawny chicken that would become dinner. Now I found myself driving a Volvo around the Boston suburbs, selecting a fat, de-feathered, beheaded, plastic-wrapped, yellow-skinned roaster at the local supermarket.

Lucas and Ila begged, nagged, and finally sweet-talked me into a series of pets: goldfish, a snake, hamsters, two cats, and a dog over the course of three years. I appreciated the lessons, especially from the two cats Perseus and Athena, and from Sophie the poodle, about loyalty, responsibility, companionship, and unconditional affection. Still, Frank, Lucas and Ila, Perseus, Athena, and Sophie became a pack, while I watched their interactions from the sidelines. After Lucas and Ila grew up and left home, I was happy to find another loving family for the cats. A year later, Sophie died, and is still mourned.

But I'm the guest who flinches when your cat rubs against my legs or jumps onto my lap. I'm the one who backs away when your dog comes sniffing, the one who thinks it's neurotic to be baby-talking another creature that isn't a baby. And while I never looked at our cats and dog and imagined sancocho, my neighbor's well-fed pet pig, which he claims is smart and affectionate, would make the perfect lechón en varita.

Pernil (Roasted Pork Shoulder)

When it's impossible to roast a whole pig (the lechón), Puerto Ricans make pork shoulder (pernil).

7 ½–8 ½ pounds pork shoulder roast

Sofrito

1 green pepper, quartered
1 red pepper, quartered
1 sweet Italian pepper, or 3–4 Puerto Rican ají dulce if you can find them at your supermarket (wash, dry, and remove stems and seeds, place in food processor or blender)
1 bunch cilantro washed, dried and hard stems removed
1 large yellow onion, quartered
¼ cup pitted alcaparrado (Spanish olives)
1 tablespoon capers
1 tablespoon oregano

Adobo

1 teaspoon peppercorns
8 large cloves garlic, peeled
3 teaspoons dried oregano
2 tablespoons salt or to taste
2 tablespoons olive oil
2 tablespoons vinegar

Wash and dry pork roast. Score meat all around with a sharp knife, creating deep cuts. Set aside.

Make the sofrito by combining all ingredients and processing until it forms a purée.

Then, make the adobo by mashing peppercorns, garlic, oregano, and salt in mortar and pestle until they form a paste. Add olive oil, vinegar, and sofrito until the paste is smooth.

Rub adobo over the pork, making sure paste goes deep into slits and cuts. Place pork in roasting pan skin side up.

Pour ¼ cup of the sofrito over roast, cover pan tightly with aluminum foil, and allow meat to marinate, preferably overnight.

Preheat oven to 325. Remove the pan with the pork from the refrigerator 30 minutes before cooking. Do not remove aluminum foil cover.

Cook for 5–6 hours. Carefully remove foil and raise oven temperature to 375. Cook for another hour or until skin is crisp and meat falls off the bone.

Allow meat to rest for 20 minutes before serving.

Makes 6–8 servings.

ESMERALDA SANTIAGO is the author of the acclaimed memoirs *When I Was Puerto Rican, Almost a Woman*—adapted into a film for *Masterpiece Theatre*—and *The Turkish Lover*. Her most recent book is the historical novel, *Conquistadora*.

LAURIE HOGIN
GRILLING WITH JACK

Growing up in southern Connecticut, I had a childhood friend named Jack. He wore horn-rimmed glasses and sweaters scented with mothballs and boy sweat, and we were inseparable: When we weren't in school together, we were in the woods beyond the back yard of my parents' house. A storage shed functioned as a toy depository where Jack and I stored field guides, Hot Wheels, model horses, prized rocks (southern Connecticut is surprisingly rich in fluorescent quartzite minerals), feathers, wood fungus, and bones.

On a trip to Caldor in the summer of 1971, Jack and I found a four-dollar, cast iron, miniature hibachi grill. We took it to the woods and placed it on the mossy ground behind a massive oak tree where we couldn't be seen from the house, in case anyone was looking. Firing it up

with forest litter and dry twigs, we tried to burn acorns, lichen, hickory nuts and puffballs, though we never tried to eat them. I think we also roasted some toys and household items, just to see what would happen. When we actually wanted to eat, we cooked cold cuts and leftover chicken, slathered in butter and seasoned with black pepper, garlic powder, or whatever other dried herbs we managed to pilfer from the kitchen. We were convinced we were inventing great, original recipes.

All these years later, I still have an affinity for grilled and pan-seared meats. This recipe uses wintry flavors, but the cider-maple marmalade can be varied with the seasons. For example, to minimize the sweetness, reduce the syrup and increase the vinegar, or add lemon or other bright flavors, or even try a summery dash of cayenne.

Grilled Pork Chops with Cider-Maple Marmalade

2 pounds pork chops, any type, 1–1 ½ inches thick

1 medium white or yellow onion

vegetable oil for sautéing and pan searing

¾ cup cider

3 tablespoons maple syrup

2 tablespoons soy sauce or worcestershire sauce

2 tablespoons apple cider vinegar

¼ teaspoon cloves

¼ teaspoon cinnamon

3 star anise pods

zest and juice of 1 large orange

3 tablespoons Dijon mustard (or to taste)

2 cloves garlic, chopped fine or pressed

3 tablespoons Grand Marnier

10 prunes, soaked in Grand Marnier for 3–6 hours

Whisk together cider, orange juice, syrup, soy sauce, vinegar, and spices. Add the anise pods last to minimize the possibility of breaking them. Put the meat in a container that allows for maximum immersion of meat in liquid (a freezer bag works very well) and refrigerate for 3–6 hours. Remove chops and allow them to reach room temperature, about 45 minutes to an hour depending on thickness. Pat them dry and season with pepper before cooking. Reserve liquid for marmalade.

Cook chops according to your favorite technique. Make sure meat is cooked to 145 degrees in the center but not overcooked, and have good grill marks or are nicely browned and caramel-crusted. If chops are very thick, par-bake them in a 275-degree oven for 20–30 minutes or until the internal temperature is 120 or so. Then brown them in the pan until safe temperature is reached. Let the chops rest for 10 minutes under a foil tent after cooking.

Slice onion very thin and sauté in oil over medium heat until soft, add garlic and sauté until garlic is barely cooked, translucent and only slightly brown, about 30 seconds. (If pan-searing, brown the chops in oil first, and cook the marmalade in the same pan; the brown bits from the meat add flavor to the marmalade.)

Remove anise pods and add marinade liquid to pan, increase heat, and cook until liquid has thickened and reduced to about ½ cup.

Cut soaked prunes into strips; add to marmalade mixture and cook until prunes are incorporated and heated through.

Turn off heat and stir in Dijon mustard until blended. Spoon marmalade mixture over meat and sprinkle with orange zest before serving (use orange zest to taste; it is not necessary to use all of it).

LAURIE HOGIN's allegorical paintings of mutant plants and animals in languishing, overgrown landscapes have been exhibited nationally and internationally for more than 20 years. Currently, she is Professor and Chair of the Painting and Sculpture Program in the School of Art and Design at the University of Illinois at Urbana-Champaign, where she has taught since 1997. She lives and works in rural Illinois with her husband and their teenage son.

NIKKI S. LEE
NIKKI'S EGG BIBIMBAP

Koreans sometimes say to children, *you're all grown up when you can enjoy something spicy.*

As a child, my mother often made me egg bibimbap, a simple, traditional Korean dish made of sticky rice topped with soy sauce and egg. But I hardly ever ate it plain. Instead, I used to like to add in lots of kimchi—a spicy/sour fermented cabbage—and a big spoon of spicy Korean red pepper paste. Eating a complex, spicier version of the dish made me feel like I was already becoming an adult.

Years later, I left Korea and moved to New York City to study photography at The Fashion Institute of Technology and New York University. Finally all grown up and cooking for myself, I surprised myself by longing for egg bibimbap the way my mother made it. I cooked it often in those days, usually leaving out all the spice as she once did for me.

I still prepare and eat the dish regularly, and when I do, I feel like I'm temporarily transported from the complex adult world to the simpler world of a child.

Nikki's Egg Bibimbap

2 eggs
Korean sticky white rice
gim (Korean dried seaweed)
sesame oil
soy sauce

Prepare the Korean sticky rice. If you don't have sticky rice, use any other white rice.

Fry your eggs any way you prefer (sunny side up, scrambled, etc.)

Add the prepared eggs to the rice. Then, add the gim, a dash of sesame oil, and the soy sauce, and generously mix with a spoon.

NIKKI S. LEE investigates notions of identity through the medium of photography and film. Born in South Korea, Lee subsequently moved to New York City where she studied photography at the Fashion Institute of Technology and New York University. Lee has exhibited at major institutions around the world, including solo exhibitions at The Institute of Contemporary Art, Boston; Yerba Buena Center for the Arts, San Francisco; and Museum of Contemporary Photography, Chicago. Her works are in the collections of major museums, including the Metropolitan Museum of Art, the Guggenheim Museum, The Hammer Museum at UCLA, and the Hirshhorn Museum.

KAMROOZ ARAM
THE DISTINCTIVE MELANCHOLY
OF GHORMEH SABZI

When I think about my childhood, I am often overcome with an almost debilitating sense of nostalgia. I'm sure my childhood was full of joyful moments; indeed nearly everyone who was there tells me it was. But sometimes when I think back, what I remember most is feeling a deep sadness. Some might argue that this is an essentially Iranian feeling, comparable to the Turkish notion of *hüzün*. It is in the poetry of Rumi and in the scales of Persian music: *Dastgahe Shur* or *Esfahan* or *Dashti* for example. It is the poetry of longing, which teases one gently toward fulfillment, only to leave one to find satisfaction in the beauty of emptiness, absence, and distance.

My favorite Iranian dish since childhood is called ghormeh sabzi, and for me there is something of this melancholy in this aromatic stew. My earliest memories of it involve air raid alerts and the rumbling of Iraqi bombs echoing over the city like not-so-distant thunder. My mother would proclaim, "Children, it's time for a picnic!" and we would hurry down the cool, echoing stairwell to the basement of our building in Tehran where we would eat our ghormeh sabzi under the blaring music of Googoosh and Hayedeh, which disguised, but failed to cover up, the sounds of bombs.

Ghormeh sabzi immigrated with us to the U.S., where my mother continued to make it on a regular basis, until I was away from home long enough to find the need to learn how to make it myself. This is not something I learned in one mother-son tutorial. In fact, it is something—like painting—that I have not really learned, but continue to pursue. And so what I offer to you is my best attempt at evoking this special food, which might allow you to find your path toward creating a version of it.

Ghormeh Sabzi

cooking oil
onions, chopped
lamb stew meat and shanks
turmeric
kidney beans
parsley
leeks
dried fenugreek (not fenugreek
   seeds)
salt and pepper
sun-dried limes

Ghormeh sabzi: A fragrant, dark-green stew of lamb and herbs with that unmistakable combination of sun-dried limes and fenugreek. Traditionally, preparing it is a full day's work. It is the cuisine of a culture entrenched in gender roles, one in which the heavily moustached men of the household work all day while the women stay home, preparing food, looking after the children, their babies wrapped mummy-like in a ghondagh. But while time is a critical ingredient in Iranian food, today, time is a luxury that is often not afforded to most Iranians, at home or abroad. It was not until later in life, when I started to cook, that I was perplexed by the fact that my mother—who worked long days in a variety of jobs ranging from baking to sewing at a drycleaner—managed to put this dish on the table on a regular basis.

My brother insists that chopping the herbs by hand actually tastes better than shredding them in a food processor, and I'm sure he would consider it a great victory for me to admit that he may be right. After chopping the leeks and herbs, sauté them until they "release a distinct aroma," as my mother says. You might interrupt me here and say, "This is fine, but I really don't have time to do this kind of cooking, I'm an architect, a single mom, a restless flaneur..." Here is a tip: When you are preparing your herbs, consider chopping two or even four times as much as you need. Once you have sautéed the herbs, pack them up and freeze them. Now you have cut your next ghormeh sabzi session in half. When you arrive home at 7 or so, you can begin by sautéing the onions and meat with turmeric, salt, and pepper. Then, simply take out a bag of your frozen herbs and add them to the meat.

What gives ghormeh sabzi its distinct aroma—and perhaps its distinct melancholy—are the sun-dried limes and fenugreek. Iranian sun-dried limes are brown on the outside and black on the inside. They are limes that have been stripped of their bright green color, their fresh aromatic visage drained of light, embracing a certain gloom, revealing a bitterness that some might consider an acquired taste. However, after hours of stewing, the limes relinquish this bitterness, lending only their fragrant aroma to the stew.

Crush a few of these dried limes (I put them in a dish towel and crush them under the weight of a can of kidney beans) and add them to the herbs and meat along with some water. Then stew for at least three hours. By this method, dinner will be ready before midnight. And of course this will not do, which is why one can resort to the pressure cooker. As the stew begins to come together (after 2 ½ hours on the stove or 30 minutes in the pressure cooker) you can add the fenugreek and the kidney beans for the final 30-45 minutes of stewing. While it may raise eyebrows or even stir great controversy to suggest this, I also like to add some fresh or frozen chopped spinach at this point. With the pressure cooker and the frozen pre-cooked herbs, you can have your ghormeh sabzi prepared in just 1–1 ½ hours. Unless, of course, you have not prepared the rice—but the art of preparing Iranian rice is a story for another occasion.

KAMROOZ ARAM has a diverse artistic practice that often engages the complicated relationship between traditional non-Western art and Western Modernism. His work has been exhibited internationally and has been widely featured and reviewed in numerous publications including *The New York Times, Art in America, ArtAsiaPacific,* and *Bidoun*. Aram's practice occasionally extends beyond the studio to include writing, organizing exhibitions, and teaching part-time at Parsons, The New School for Design. Born in Shiraz, Iran, Aram lives and works in Brooklyn, New York.

NIKKI GIOVANNI
ONLY A KISS

I lived with my grandparents in Knoxville, Tennessee. Grandpapa taught Latin at Austin High and Grandmother substituted teaching but mostly she cooked for the school and for other folk. We were not poor but no one could call us rich either. In those days, education had a lot to do with how you perceived yourself and how you were perceived by others.

Holidays were important to us. We didn't do a lot for Christmas but being Christians, Baptist actually, Easter meant a lot because "He rose on Easter." My job was to wash and iron and clean the house. Grandmother cooked, and Grandpapa kept us company by telling stories. His favorite meal on any holiday except the 4th of July was roast rack of lamb. He did the shopping, so he would go to market to purchase the rack, and then

Grandmother would start her preparation. And all the while, I got to hear stories about how they met and how he courted her.

"You know, Nikki," he would start, "I only wanted to kiss your grandmother." And she would chime in from the kitchen, "John Brown, if I had let you kiss me you would never have married me." Grandparents, I thought, are strange; I didn't know that "kiss" was a word for something else. "I would walk down the street, pass her house to see if she was out," he would continue. "John Brown," she would laugh, "you were already married. You had married that Spelman girl and I knew better than to talk with you." I was thinking, why wouldn't she talk with him? He told good stories and was lots of fun. "I asked my friend to invite you out for ice cream. And you would come." "Well, yes, because I love ice cream but I brought my girl friend along so that we would never be alone." "I thought that was terrible of you…" "I told your friend that I liked you and was sorry you were married." "Nikki, after a while I realized she was very stubborn, and I was not going to get a kiss until I got a divorce. My family was upset, but I did the right thing. Without that divorce, I couldn't have had your aunts and your mother. That's important because that's how we got you."

I used to look at them laughing with each other. I decided I would learn to cook and I already knew how to clean but I knew I was never going to get married. There were too many questions. Of course, now I understand that Grandpapa was talking "dirty" to Grandmother in front of me. I still think of those stories when I roast my own rack of lamb, and smile at the love that lasted for the rest of their lives.

Smoked Rack of Lamb

olive oil
rack of lamb
garlic
rosemary
thyme
tarragon
nutmeg

First, start with good meat. To thaw, I put it in a glass dish with a comfortable blanket of olive oil. That way, as it unthaws it gets a drink. I like garlic so I peel and cut a small head and put it on the rack. Then rosemary, thyme, tarragon, and, of course, a sharing of nutmeg. A bit more olive oil, too.

Soak the wood chips in a small bucket of water then light the fire. After about 15 minutes, when the coals are white, put the rack on. Let it brown til it's a bit charred then turn it over. Brown yet again. Add the wood chips which will cause the charcoal to smoke. Put the rack to one side and add the top to the grill. Smoke will come from the top.

Drink a glass of champagne while keeping an eye on the lamb. By the time you finish your drink, turn the rack over. Let it smoke for about 10 minutes more. You can test it with a knife but it should be done.

If it's summer, boil bi-colored corn; if winter, make creamed peas, and add a nice green salad at either time. We're ready for dinner with laughter and friends. No friends? Then red wine for sure. Now we're ready.

NIKKI GIOVANNI is a poet who was born in Knoxville, Tennessee, on June 7, 1943. She is the author of three *New York Times* and *Los Angeles Times* Best Sellers and has won numerous awards, including seven NAACP Image Awards and the Langston Hughes Medal. Since 1987, she has been on the faculty at Virginia Tech, where she is a University Distinguished Professor.

RUTH OZEKI
MEAT

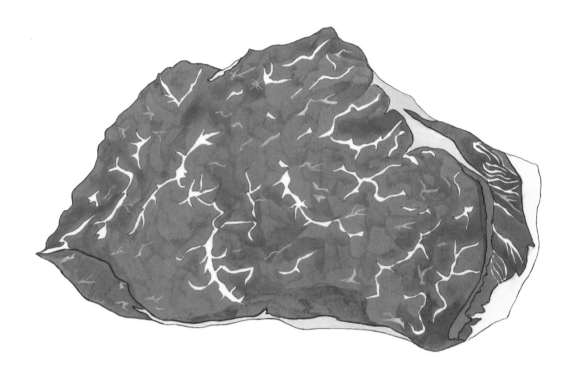

One good thing about being a novelist is that nothing is wasted. Every silly thing you've ever done—every mistake, dumb job, bad idea, failed relationship—is redeemed by its novelistic potential.

Something that fell into the dumb-job/bad-idea category was a cooking show I once produced for Japanese TV. The show was called *Mrs. America*, and in spite of its somewhat regressive title, the idea—to profile diverse American women leading interesting personal and professional lives—seemed quite forward-thinking. It was the 1980s, a time when Japanese women enjoyed fewer freedoms than they do today, and when she married, a woman was expected to leave the workplace and became a mother and a housewife, rather than pursuing a career. The hope of our young, New York-based production team of gung-ho professional woman

was that the show might inspire our sisters in Japan. I pitched the idea to the production company, and they found a network, and later a sponsor: an American meat industry lobby group. The sponsor wanted to inspire Japanese housewives, too. They wanted to inspire them to buy American beef.

We got the green light and went ahead with the show. My job was to travel all over the United States with a Japanese television crew, filming American housewives cooking delicious recipes for beef. We documented all manner of wives and meats, and I became quite knowledgeable about tenderloins and strip steaks, ribs and rumps, briskets and T-bones. Later, after I got out of the TV business, this experience proved to be extremely inspiring to me, as well. It inspired me to write my first novel, *My Year of Meats*.

Here is a recipe from that novel. I learned a version of it from a real housewife in Florida, although in the novel it's prepared by a fictional housewife named Suzie Flowers.

When you were a kid, did you ever do that experiment where you put a tooth in a glass of Coca-Cola before you go to bed, and when you wake up in the morning, the tooth is gone? The point is to prove that Coca-Cola dissolves teeth so you shouldn't drink it, but it also illustrates why Coca-Cola makes such a good meat tenderizer: it breaks down muscle fiber, and makes even a lesser cut of meat quite delicious—tender, succulent, and sweet.

Coca-Cola Roast

2 kilograms American beef (rump roast)
1 can Campbell's Cream of Mushroom Soup
1 package Lipton's Powdered Onion Soup
1.5 liters Coca-Cola (not Pepsi, please!)

Preheat the oven to 250.

Put the roast in a roasting pan. Mix the ingredients together and pour over the meat.

Cover tightly with a lid or with aluminum foil. Cook for three hours, or until done.

RUTH OZEKI is a novelist, filmmaker, and Zen Buddhist priest. Her award-winning novels, *My Year of Meats, All Over Creation,* and most recently *A Tale for the Time Being,* have been translated and published in over 30 countries. She is the Elizabeth Drew Professor of Creative Writing at Smith College, and she splits her time between Massachusetts, New York, and Whaletown, British Columbia.

ALEXIS ROCKMAN
WHAT DOROTHY ORDERED

On the last day of a road trip to Santa Fe and the Grand Canyon, Dorothy, my partner, insisted that we go out to lunch at Cafe Pasqual's in Santa Fe. I remember the restaurant had a welcoming, hippy-cowboy vibe, but I actually can't remember a thing about what I ordered because I was so distracted by what Dorothy ordered— grilled skirt steak berbere. I had instant food envy. The smell was aromatic and exotic, as if it contained the perfect combination of the world's greatest spices. She wouldn't let me try any, so I just inhaled the aromas, longing for a taste. Since then, I've learned to just copy whatever Dorothy orders every time we go out to eat.

As we were leaving, I saw they had a cookbook, which I bought for Dorothy. Although as it turns out, I bought it mostly for me; I'm the only one who cooks from it, and I only cook one thing.

Despite having discovered this recipe by way of Santa Fe, grilled skirt steak berbere actually has Ethiopian origins.

Bebere is a spice blend that's an essential component of Ethiopian cuisine. It has many variations but it's always intensely hot and rich, and can include chili peppers, sweet paprika, fenugreek, ginger, garlic, turmeric, cardamom, coriander, nutmeg, salt, black pepper, as well as other spices that were once unfamiliar to me: korarima, rue, ajwain, and nigella. You can buy the spices individually, as I do (just combine all ingredients in a blender and blend it—the smell and flavor is incredible), or, if you prefer, purchase as a spice blend, which is easier, but the taste doesn't come close.

My version of the recipe has been adapted, with thanks, from the Cafe Pasqual's cookbook. I've made it in snow boots in the dead of the winter, and for everyone including my son's high school basketball team and visiting art dealer that I work with. They all enjoy it. Served alongside an arugula salad with blue cheese dressing, it has become one of our favorite meals.

Grilled Skirt Steak Berbere

½ cup olive oil
½ cup lime juice
¼ cup berbere spice (more to taste)
3 tablespoons pressed garlic
2 teaspoons kosher salt
2 pounds skirt steak
2 limes, cut into wedges

Combine all ingredients except steak into bowl and mix. Add steak to bowl and mix and marinate, refrigerated, for a minimum of 8 hours (and up to 2 days).

Grill for 2 minutes a side over an open grill with wood charcoal.

ALEXIS ROCKMAN has depicted a darkly surreal vision of the collision between civilization and nature—often apocalyptic paintings on a monumental scale—for over three decades. The first survey of Rockman's paintings and works on paper, "Alexis Rockman: A Fable for Tomorrow," was presented in 2010–2011 at the Smithsonian American Art Museum. In 2011, Rockman collaborated with filmmaker Ang Lee, creating conceptual sketches and designing a sequence for the Academy Award winning film, *Life of Pi.* His art is in the public collections of numerous museums including the Whitney Museum in New York and the Hammer Museum in Los Angeles. He lives and works in New York.

T.C. BOYLE
BAKED CAMEL (STUFFED)

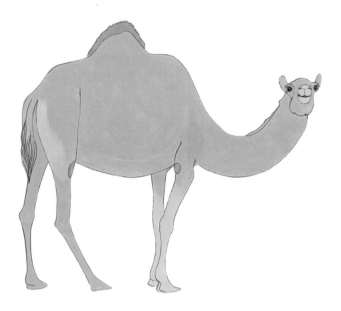

What can I say about this recipe, except to offer a gentle admonition: This is for a very large party. And yes, it's a lot of work, what with digging the trench, de-hiding the sheep and camel, plucking the bustards, and scaling the carp, but it's worth it, believe me. Or don't believe me.

Various versions of this recipe were floating around when I was a student at the Iowa Writers' Workshop and attempting my first novel, *Water Music*, from the pages of which this has been extracted. I was pretty hungry at the time, living on a student's income and what little I then made from writing ($25.00 from the *North American Review*, where I published my first story, and which bought a whole lot of beer in Iowa City in those days), and I suppose I went a bit overboard on this particular recipe, thinking of that delectable trench-roasted camel flank and the steaming, glutinous, faintly fishy (and sheepy) flesh of those stuffed bustards, but so be it. When you think large, you eat large.

Baked Camel (Stuffed)

500 dates
200 plover eggs
20 2-pound carp
4 bustards, cleaned and plucked
2 sheep
1 large camel
seasonings

Dig trench. Reduce inferno to hot coals, three feet in depth. Separately hard-cook eggs. Scale carp and stuff with shelled eggs and dates. Season bustards and stuff with stuffed carp. Stuff stuffed bustards into sheep and stuffed sheep into camel. Singe camel. Then wrap in leaves of doum palm and bury in pit. Bake two days. Serve with rice.

T. CORAGHESSAN BOYLE is the author of 25 books of fiction, most recently *The Harder They Come* (2015), *T.C. Boyle Stories II* (2013), *San Miguel* (2012), *When the Killing's Done* (2011), *Wild Child* (2010), and *The Women* (2009). He is a member of the American Academy of Arts and Letters and lives in Santa Barbara, California.

ELIZABETH ALEXANDER
ADULIS

When Ficre Ghebreyesus and I met in met in New Haven in the late spring of 1996, the first thing he wanted to do was show me his art. He was living at the time at 218 State Street, the New Haven Cash Register Company building, in an unfinished loft where he slept and painted when he was not cooking his Eritrean fantasia food in the kitchen of Caffé Adulis, the restaurant he owned and ran with his brothers Gideon and Sahle. The restaurant was named in homage to Adulis, an ancient port city on the Red Sea that is now an archaeological excavation site, one of Africa's great "lost cities." Pliny the Elder was the first writer to mention Adulis, which he called "city of free men."

In those days Ficre used to chef through the evening, close down the restaurant, then paint until dawn in that loft, with its salvaged Steinway piano, a clothing rack he'd rolled down the street from Macy's when it went out of business and used as a closet for his few hanging garments, and graffiti scrawled by a previous occupant on the heavy metal door that read, "Foster Kindness."

There were paintings everywhere, mostly large dark canvases lit with brilliant corners of insistent life. The paintings gave a sense of his beloved homeland in wartime—the Eritrean War of Independence began shortly before he was born—infused with the light of determined humanity that would not be deferred or

→

extinguished. He showed me pastel drawings with the driving color concerns that echoed Eritrean textile work and basketry as well as Matisse's sky-lit hues. There were linocuts and mono-prints he'd made at the Printmaking Workshop with master teacher Bob Blackburn, and paintings he'd made while studying at the Art Students League with Joseph Stapleton, one of the last of the Abstract Expressionists then teaching. Ficre made that art during New York years in which he was mostly working as a young people's leader and activist on behalf of Eritrean issues. And then there were portfolios of photographs—some of which would be exhibited at an office building of the U.S. Congress that summer—which told stories of Eritrea and its uncannily resilient people in saturated, painterly colors.

As Ficre showed me work he talked about his family: his late father, Gebreyesus Tessema, a judge so ethical he was exiled hundreds of miles away from home when he refused to tamper with his judicial decisions to suit the wishes of the dictator and minions. He adhered to many formalities and customs, Ficre said, but also loved his children—seven in total, one, Kebede, lost to war, Ficre at the number-six position—to climb on him and laugh when all would come home from work and school for the midday meal.

His mother, Zememesh Berhe, also navigated the family ship through the vagaries of war. She came from a clan of many sisters and one brother, respected and tough Coptic Christian highlanders, who all raised their children near each other until war scattered them and took some of their lives. Mama Zememesh had Parkinson's disease, he told me that first day, and all of his siblings—Tadu, Mehret, Sara, Gideon, and Sahle, then in Addis Ababa, Nairobi, and New Haven, doted on her as she moved from one family constellation to

the next. Their language was Tigrinya, an Afro-Asiatic tongue derived from the ancient South Semitic Ge'ez and spoken in Eritrea and its diaspora. His full name, Ficremariam Ghebreyesus, means "lover of Mary" and "servant of Jesus." The abbreviated "Ficre," as he was called, means "love."

Our love began in an instant and progressed inevitably. When Solomon Kebede Ghebreyesus, our first son, was born in April of 1998, we moved to 45 Livingston Street in New Haven. Ficre continued to invent and cook at Adulis. The great food writer and old-school newspaperman R.W. Apple visited the restaurant and after tasting Ficre's creations asked, in his article in *The New York Times,* "A Culinary Journey out of Africa and into New Haven":

"Is all of this authentic?"...

"Tricky word, authentic," [Ficre] replied. "Tricky idea. Food ideas move around the world very quickly today, and if you went to Eritrea, you'd find American touches here and there. There are thousands of Eritreans living in the United States, and when they go home, they take new food ideas with them. For us, that's no more foreign than pasta once was."

Adulis was a gathering place where people ate food they'd never imagined and learned about the culture and history of a country that most of them had never heard of. Ficre created legendary dishes such as shrimp barka that existed nowhere in Eritrea but rather in his own inventive imagination. Women called for it from St. Raphael's and Yale-New Haven Hospitals after they'd delivered their babies; people said they literally dreamed of it, a fairy food that tasted like nothing else. Here is how you make it.

Shrimp Barka

4 tablespoons olive oil

3 medium red onions, thinly sliced

4–6 cloves garlic, minced

5 very ripe and juicy tomatoes, chopped coarsely

salt and freshly ground black pepper, to taste

½ cup finely chopped fresh basil (1 bunch)

15 pitted dates (½ cup), cut crosswise in thirds

3 tablespoons unsweetened shredded coconut

½ cup half-and-half

1 pound medium shrimp (16–20), shelled and deveined

⅔ cup grated Parmesan cheese

2 ½ cups cooked basmati rice

In a large, heavy pot, heat olive oil over medium heat. Add onions, and sauté until wilted, about 10 minutes. Add garlic, and continue sautéing, stirring frequently to prevent sticking, for 2 minutes longer. Stir in the tomatoes, salt, and pepper. Cover, and cook for about 5 minutes.

Add basil, dates, and coconut, and reduce heat to medium-low. Cook uncovered, stirring occasionally, for 5 more minutes. Add the half-and-half, cover, and cook for 3 minutes.

Add shrimp to sauce. Cook covered, until shrimp turn pink, about 5 minutes. Stir in cheese and then the rice, and serve immediately.

ELIZABETH ALEXANDER is a poet, essayist, and teacher. She is the author of six books of poems, two collections of essays, a play, a memoir, and various edited collections. She was recently named a Chancellor of the Academy of American Poets, as well as the Wun Tsun Tam Mellon Professor in the Humanities at Columbia University. In 2009, she composed and delivered "Praise Song for the Day" for the inauguration of President Barack Obama.

PETER HO DAVIES
AUTHENTIC SINGAPORE CHILLI CRAB

Like many who enjoy ethnic or international food, I like to think the dishes I'm eating are authentic: "real" Indian, or Mexican, or Italian, etc. But while I question the bona fides of many cuisines, the issue seems especially knotty when it comes to my own ancestral ethnic food: Chinese. From its start during the Gold Rush years in California, after all, U.S. Chinese food was popular with and produced for a largely non-Chinese clientele of hungry white prospectors and their hangers-on. What resulted was a Chinese cuisine adapted to Western palates, and to some extent available western ingredients. Chop suey is widely believed to be one such Chinese American invention; fortune cookies another. You could argue, in fact, that Chinese American food predates Chinese-Americans given that the earliest Chinese in America saw themselves more as sojourners rather than immigrants, and America, via various exclusion acts, sought for decades to ensure that Chinese didn't settle in the country.

Now, I'm half-Chinese by blood, but, brought up in the West, I'm probably considerably less than half-Chinese culturally. Food has been a large part of my meager Chinese acculturation, but much of it—sweet and sour pork, special fried rice, egg rolls—has necessarily been Western Chinese food. Delicious? Sure. Authentic? Not so much. My own uncertainty about how authentically Chinese I am is thus reflected in the food that I love.

When I travelled to Malaysia, where my Chinese family hail from, as well as nearby Singapore, I found my relatives liked to put my Chineseness to the test—mostly in a good-natured way—by seeing if I could "take" the local food, everything from bird's nest soup to thousand year old eggs to sea cucumber. Some I liked, some I hated and pretended to like, but one I loved was Singapore chilli crab. Hot, sweet, and messy—some Singaporean's crack the shells with their teeth at hawker markets—it's not a common restaurant dish in the West, so I was excited to learn a surprisingly quick and simple recipe for it, and even more excited to learn that this quintessentially Asian dish utilizes a quintessentially Western ingredient—tomato ketchup. (The word "ketchup" itself has a Chinese or possibly Malay root, and refers to a fish sauce, but the tomato variety seems deeply American). In Singapore restaurants, by the way, chilli crab is usually served with a side of soft white bread, another atypical ingredient in Chinese dishes, but just the thing to mop up the rich red sauce.

Authentic Singapore Chilli Crab
(serves 2 in about 15 minutes)

2 crab clusters (Dungeness for preference, though snow or king crab is just fine)
2 cloves chopped garlic
1 inch grated ginger
2 tablespoons oil
⅓ cup ketchup
⅓ cup sugar
⅓ cup water
3–4 healthy squirts Sriracha hot sauce
1 bunch chopped scallions
1 egg, beaten
soft white bread, cubed

Break the legs off the crab clusters, and snap at joints. Separate the body into 2 or 3 chunks with a cleaver. Crab legs should also be pre-cracked with the edge of the cleaver (or cracker). Mix ketchup, sugar, and water.

Fry the garlic and ginger in the oil in a large wok.

Add the crab legs and body and stir fry for 3–5 minutes (or until crab meat turns white).

Add Sriracha sauce (3–4 squirts, or more to taste), then add mixture of ketchup, sugar, and water and simmer for 5 minutes.

Mix in beaten egg to thicken.

Serve garnished with chopped scallions, and bread for dipping in sauce.

Eat with your hands, with someone you don't mind getting messy with.

PETER HO DAVIES is the author of the novels, *The Fortunes* and *The Welsh Girl,* and two story collections, *The Ugliest House in the World* and *Equal Love.* His work has appeared in *Harpers, The Atlantic,* and *The Paris Review,* and been anthologized in *Prize Stories: The O. Henry Awards* and *Best American Short Stories.* In 2003 *Granta* magazine named him among its "Best of Young British Novelists." Born in England to Welsh and Chinese parents, Davies now lives in the U.S. and teaches in the MFA Program at the University of Michigan.

ANN CRAVEN
LET THE LOBSTERS GO

When I was a little girl, I used to sneak out to the kitchen and let the lobsters go. My uncle John would sometimes help me do this—he always knew my secrets, and he taught me how to break the rules, but in a good way. He would say, we can let one go, but I always tried for at least two or three.

I grew up in Boston but my family spent summers in Seabrook, New Hampshire with my uncle John, in his big weathered white house on the beach side of the street. I loved the old house, even though (or perhaps especially because) I thought it had ghosts. In the daytime, my uncle and I would go looking for buried treasures; at night, my mom prepared lobster dinners for the whole family. We all loved lobster and ate it like pros; nothing was left behind.

Although I enjoyed the meal as much as everyone else in my family, watching dinner transition from living to dead was hard for me. So, I took matters into my own hands. Sometimes, rather than smuggle them out of the

kitchen—tricky business, even with my uncle as partner-in-crime—I tried to convince my mother to let me keep the lobsters as pets. I had lots of other animals already: a dog, a raccoon, a rabbit, a snake. What possible difference could a few little lobsters make? Of course my mom never allowed me to keep any, though I think she knew of my secret lobster rescues and planned our dinners accordingly, pretending to lose count.

I remember grabbing the lobster and pulling the wooden dowel out—*fast!*—that was lodged inside the claw to keep them from fighting while in their holding tanks. Then, lobster in hand, I would run to the sea and throw them back in, gently but swiftly, always trying to do it as fast as possible so that I wouldn't get caught. The tail would be flipping out of control, claws flailing, until finally I'd hear that small splash. Relief.

Of course, I never did let them *all* go. Here is my favorite recipe for the ones that didn't get away.

Steamed Lobster, New England Style

1–1½ pound lobsters—hard or soft shell (hard shell have more meat but can take a lot of work to get the meat out)
butter, melted (unsalted or salted)
water
salt

To cook your lobsters, you'll need a 3–4 gallon pasta pot for 5 lobsters, and/or larger pot if you are cooking more than 5. Put three inches of water in the pot and add a steamer rack. Bring the water to a roaring hard boil, then add the lobsters in the water "backside first" so that they are on their backs upon entering the scalding water. (This position helps keep the green tomalley in place, and not drive it up into the tail. My family loved the tomalley and ate it with a spoon.)

Place about 5 lobsters in this pot—one at a time, fast—or as many will fit in the pot. For the record, it still pains me to see the lobsters cook, and I usually enlist anyone near to me to do the deed. So, do what you need to do, then cover the pot with a tight fitting lid!

Return to a boil and steam until the lobster is bright red, about 12–14 minutes (do not over-cook).

Pull at the antennae; if they pull out easily, the lobsters are done.

Remove the lobsters from the pot and place each one on old-fashioned plastic school lunch trays (these trays are easier to clean and store) along with an ear of fresh, local, cooked corn and some coleslaw.

Serve with small bowls of melted butter for dipping.

ANN CRAVEN is known for her bold portraits of flowers, birds, deer, the moon, and her paintings with stripes of color. Born in Boston, Craven studied at Massachusetts College of Art and Columbia University. Her paintings have been exhibited internationally and are in the public collections of museums including the Whitney Museum and MoMA. Currently, she divides her time between New York City and Maine, where she has been painting the moon since the late 1990s.

LEV GROSSMAN
PAN-SEARED SCALLOPS WITH BÉARNAISE SAUCE AND A WHOLE NEW LIFE

You'll want to set aside some time for this. The pan-seared scallops are quick: you put them in a pan and sear them. The Béarnaise sauce takes a little more time and care. And getting ready to start a new life takes about 35 years. Or it did for me, anyway.

Start by neglecting yourself—that's the 35 years. Nothing dramatic, just be a little lazy. Don't write the book you want to write. Don't get therapy when you're depressed. Don't eat nice things like scallops or Béarnaise sauce, or do any of the other things that might give you pleasure. Instead, live a dull, cold, under-pleasured life.

After a few decades of this, your brain will be like a darkened city. Imagine a whole metropolis that's wired for electricity, but there has never been any power. The entire population has just been sitting in the dark all this time, waiting.

Let them sit. You've got Béarnaise sauce to make.

Pan-Seared Scallops with Béarnaise Sauce

¼ cup fresh tarragon, chopped
2 shallots, minced
5 peppercorns, black as the devil, mercilessly crushed
¼ cup champagne vinegar

¼ cup dry white wine
3 egg yolks
1 stick butter
salt and pepper, to taste
scallops

First melt your butter, slowly, and when a little white stuff forms on the surface skim it off—that's just the milk solids. You can put the butter through a strainer if you want to be extra-fancy. When you're done, let it cool down a little. Now it's clarified butter. Is there clarity coming into your life too? Who knows. Wait and see.

Now mince and chop your shallot and your tarragon—world's most underrated herb—and stick them in a small saucepan with your vinegar, your wine, and your peppercorns. Boil that whole mess down to about a tablespoon or so. Let that cool a bit. Now whisk your egg yolks into it over very low heat, just a whisper of blue flame, so that the yolks don't actually cook, they just get a little thicker.

When that's done you can take it off the heat and gradually add your clarified butter to it in a thin golden stream, still whisking while you pour. This is the crucial step. You're working with both hands here, pouring and whisking, and your whisking hand is going to get tired, but don't stop. Whisk through the pain. If you don't, the sauce can break. Don't stop until it thickens into a proper sauce.

Thick enough? Good. Now squeeze some lemon into it, throw in some salt and pepper and a little extra chopped tarragon and you're done. That's Béarnaise sauce, and it's amazing. But wait, did you remember to neglect your own life for a few decades? Good. This next step depends on it.

Heat up a frying pan with a little olive oil in it, maybe a little butter if you're throwing caution to the wind. Get the pan hot, then throw in one single scallop. Let it sear on one side 'til there's a hint of brown crust, then flip and do the other side—maybe 90 seconds each side, no more. It's not an exact science, you can eat these things raw as sashimi anyway.

OK, scallop done? Don't bother plating it, just spear it with a fork straight out of the pan and dunk it in the Béarnaise sauce. Submerge it entirely, don't stint yourself. Now pull it out and stick it straight in your mouth. Notice that it's sour and sweet and salty and creamy, all at the same time. Notice that it's the greatest thing you've ever tasted.

Remember that city? Suddenly, for the first time ever, somebody plugs in the main line, and in an instant, the city is ablaze with light, and you're experiencing a kind of pleasure you've never known before. You've made something for yourself, you've done something for yourself—a small thing that makes you happy. Keep going. Keep doing that, forever.

LEV GROSSMAN is the author of five novels, including the international bestseller *Codex* and the #1 *New York Times* bestselling "Magicians" trilogy. The "Magicians" books have been published in 25 countries, and a Syfy series based on the trilogy premiered in early 2016. Grossman is also the book critic for *Time* magazine, and has won several awards for journalism, including a Deadline award. Born and raised in Lexington, Massachusetts, he lives in Brooklyn with his wife, two daughters, and one son.

PAUL MULDOON
A RECIPE FOR DISASTER

Take one pork cutlet,
preferably from a pig that's been growth hormone-addled
and shows evidence of low-dose antibiotics
that's sometimes swept under the rug.
Brush with a corn derivative
and place on grill.
Add two ammonia treated defatted beef patties
but only if they carry a USDA stamp.
On no account overcook
lest you accidentally kill
any of the superbugs
or other strains of bacteria about to enter your system.
It's best if they're resistant to drugs.

Take one Arctic apple
designed by the irresistible
Okanagan Specialty Fruits Inc. of Canada
to itself "resist" browning when sliced.
Cut in half
and place on grill.
Set aside your suspicion that genetic
modification is now endemic
and season with verbiage that comes by hook or by crook
from Capitol Hill.
Turn the cutlet twice,
then drizzle with honey and low pesticide residue nutmeg.
For nutmeg you may substitute low pesticide residue allspice.

Vis-à-vis the honey,
the ideal would be to harvest it from the collapsing colony
of neonicotinoid-
compromised bees
that had built some semblance of a hive
in your grill.
In a pan sweat a small onion but don't
for a moment succumb to pathogen-paranoia.
Garnish with watercress almost certainly rife with liver fluke,
raised as it was in a hydroponic rill
that's the runoff from a piggery.
As to whether the Arctic apple is "truly non-browning,"
you'll have to wait and see.

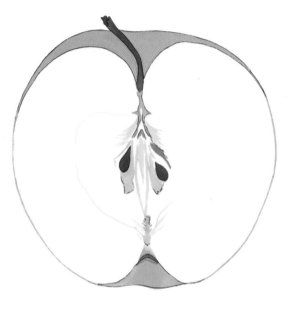

PAUL MULDOON is an Irish poet and Pulitzer Prize winner, as well as an editor, critic, and translator. He is the author of 12 books of poetry, most recently *One Thousand Things Worth Knowing* (FSG, 2015). He has also published innumerable smaller collections, works of criticism, opera libretti, books for children, song lyrics, and radio and television drama. In addition to teaching at Princeton University and serving as poetry editor of *The New Yorker*, he cooks up a storm.

ROZ CHAST
DINNERTIME

ROZ CHAST began working for *The New Yorker* less than a year out of college, and the magazine has published her cartoons continuously ever since. Her work has also appeared in *Scientific American, The Harvard Business Review,* and many other magazines. She is the author of numerous books, including *Can't We Talk about Something More Pleasant?* (2014), which received the National Book Critics Circle Award for autobiography and was a finalist for the National Book Award. Chast lives in Connecticut with her husband and two parrots.

SNACKS

ELISSA SCHAPPELL
THE CONQUEROR'S CANAPÉS

In a perfect world I'd farm my own snails. I'd play Serge Gainsbourg records and read them Catullus whilst they grazed on beds of flowering thyme and sipped the tears I've shed over my once beautiful garden, devoured under darkness by slugs—the snail's tragically inedible cousin (ironically toxic thanks to the banquet of poisons I've laid out for them, and which they seem immune to). But it's not a perfect world. In truth, I don't possess the strength of character that free-range snail farming requires nor the physical space, and not to put too fine of a point on it, but I would rather hunt and eat the ones killed on my own land.

I believe that if you're going to eat something you ought to have the decency to kill it yourself. Fight it to the death. You like steak? Then wrestle that steer to his knees. In this case, *you eat my family's tree, I'll eat yours.* Luckily all that small land-snail hunting requires is nightfall and a decent flashlight. Note that a good light rain will draw snails out in droves. As will the sound of a gardener weeping over a decimated dogwood tree.

I'd like to believe that these lowly marauders, taunting me with their silver trails of slime on my garden walls, would be pained to see that I'm eating their kin—that the sight of me forking the hot, wet-with-butter and fully parsleyed bodies of their brethren into my maw would cause them alarm. I'd like to think that if they had mouths they would cry out, if they had fists they would shake them at me, and that barring that they would retract their eye stalks and hurl themselves against the cold, hard ground until their shells splintered in protest. But they don't. They are heartless.

For the past 20 or so odd years, my husband and I have thrown a dinner party to celebrate the beginning of spring. Along with wearing flowers in our hair and rolling empty wine bottles for luck, it's become a tradition for us to serve escargot. Every year there will be a guest who, pale and trembling, delights me with their confession that they have never had snails before. What an enormous pleasure it is to be the one to give them their first taste. Until the day when I launch my fleet of *Escar-Go-Go* food carts with go-go dancers in snail pasties, making your own will have to suffice.

This recipe is adapted from one that my mother used to make every year for my father's birthday. For the record, my father was an exceptional gardener who never suffered the kind of abuse that I have from so low on the food chain. My mother's recipe presents snails at their best, no red wine, no breadcrumbs, no grated cheese, just snails and gobs of herb-besotted butter. If Venus made snails, this is how she'd prepare them.

Escargot Canapés

snails
¼ cup white wine
½ cup sea-salted water
2 cloves garlic (or to taste),
    quartered
rosemary, thyme, and marjoram
    arranged into a bouquet de garni
    (although given the small number
    of snails, this is more nosegay
    than bouquet)
butter, half a stick
small handful parsley
minced garlic, to taste
sea salt and white pepper
french bread
tiny silver forks or toothpicks
    for serving

Any decent grocery store should have snails. As for the shells, buy them. Trust me. Specialty food stores are likely to carry them; look in the neighborhood of the smoked clams. Sometimes you can find them as part of a kit with a tin of snails. Lucky you. The shells can be used over and over again and with care can be passed down for generations. I have inherited some of my mother's shells from the 70s—very retro—and I treasure them. What you don't need is the escargot pan, with its sweet, perfectly-sized depressions. A muffin tin or another tin with an edge that will keep the snaily darlings from tipping over and giving up their butters will suffice. That said, do consider making the leap to an escargot pan; when it's not in service, it doubles nicely as a palette for watercolors.

The night before serving, open your can of snails and drain them.

Transfer them into the lovely fragrant bath you've prepared of the wine, salted water, chopped garlic, and herbs. Then, cover them up, and put them in the fridge to sit overnight. When ready to serve, remove the snails from the fridge, drain the bath, and gently pat the snails dry.

I once worked in a French restaurant where the chef had us prick the snails with a pin before we stuffed them in the shells, out of a fear that they would explode. So, if you are the sort of person who worries about these kind of accidents, prick your snails with a pin.

Cream together the butter, chopped parsley, finely minced garlic, salt, and white pepper. If you want only a hint of garlic, rub a naked clove on the inside of the bowl you are using to prepare the butter mixture.

Tuck each snail, pricked or unpricked, into its own little shell and then generously cap it with your butter mixture.

Some people sprinkle cognac over the shells before they go in the oven; others a splash of Ricard. I don't think they need either.

Bake until the butter sizzles.

If you don't have tiny forks nestled in velvet and crammed in a drawer somewhere, toothpicks, while of course not as elegant, will do in a pinch, and as always, eating with your fingers has its coarse charms. Just beware—they are hot. Some people like to use what we call "snail tongs," equipment not unlike pliers and meant to hold the snail in place so you can liberate it of its meat without burning yourself or soaking your cuffs in butter.

Serve with French bread—if you're eating with your hands you will absolutely need the bread to mop the butter from your fingers. There are some people who will argue that the best part of escargot is the butter soaked bread, and who am I to argue?

ELISSA SCHAPPELL is the author of two books of fiction, *Blueprints for Building Better Girls* and *Use Me,* a runner up for the PEN/Hemingway award. She is a Contributing Editor at *Vanity Fair,* a Founding Editor, now Editor-at-Large of *Tin House* magazine and teaches in the MFA Creative Writing Program at Columbia University. Her work has appeared in numerous publications including *The Paris Review, The New York Times Book Review,* and *One Story,* and anthologies such as *The Mrs. Dalloway Reader* and *Bound to Last.* She lives in Brooklyn.

ANA CASTILLO
TÍA FLORA'S KITCHEN

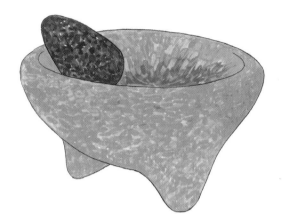

The best cook I knew growing up was not my mamá (she had a "salty hand"), nor my abuelita (from the turn of the century her recipes were constrained to the days of La Revolución: tortillas and beans and more tortillas and beans). It was my mamá's sister, Tía Flora, born in Mexico City, who learned to cook as a girl working as a domestic and had a gift for whipping up the best meals north of her birthplace.

Tía Flora had a festive personality. She sang on key as she bustled about her tiny kitchen with molcajete on hand—a stone mortar and pestle used since the Conquest—sipping a homemade Margarita out of a Martini glass. It was the early 60s. Richard Burton and Liz Taylor had just married for the first time; María Felix, the Mexican actress, considered by Paris *Vogue* to be the most beautiful woman in the world, was making her greatest movies. Glamour was in the air. In Tía Flora's barrio kitchen, chiles grilled on the comal to be peeled for sauce. All of us children ran around as Tía Flora whistled to the crooning of her favorite idols on the HiFi while conjuring up a three course meal.

There are many recipes that Tía Flora passed on to me that I never mastered near her level. But she did teach me one simple appetizer that goes well with cocktails: jicama.

Jicama

jicama
lime juice
chili powder

Also known as Mexican turnip, the jicama has the refreshing texture of an apple or water chestnut. To pick out the best jicama, the rounder and firmer the better.

Wash like a potato; keep in cool place. When ready to serve, cut off the top and bottom and peel with a paring knife. Slice and arrange on a platter.

Add lime juice and your favorite chili powder.

Put on a mambo record and don't forget the margarita pitcher. Carry out to the patio or balcony. Watch the sunset. Thank the gods for the bountiful gifts that come in the forms of roots and cacti. My ancestors didn't have it all wrong.

ANA CASTILLO is a celebrated Chicana poet, novelist, short story writer, essayist, playwright, translator, and independent scholar. She is editor of *La Tolteca*, an arts and literary journal dedicated to the advancement of a world without borders and censorship. Her award winning, best-selling novels include *So Far from God, The Guardians,* and *Peel My Love like an Onion.* Castillo's most recent book, *Black Dove (Paloma Negra): Essays on Mi'jo, Mamá and Me,* was released in May 2016.

PATRICIA MARX
ROLLED MUSHROOM CANAPÉS

When I was a kid my parents threw parties at which they served scrumptious hors d'oeuvres and candy (also stacks of cigarettes on trays but that was no concern to a child). After changing into our pajamas, my brother, sister, and I were allowed to sample the goodies in exchange for saying hello to the guests. This was no small price. Today kids may consider grownups their assistants, but back then, we thought of them as autocrats from another planet—dangerous but tedious creatures to be avoided except if you needed a ride somewhere. If it were not for the mushroom rolls and the chocolate turtles, I doubt I would have come out of my room.

The secret to these canapés is that they are really just a vehicle for moving butter into your mouth. Indeed, saturated fat and salt is the key to cooking for others—that, and never revealing the ingredients. But I will tell you.

Rolled Mushroom Canapés

10 slices white bread
butter
sour cream
½ pound mushrooms
¼ cup chopped chives and scallions
⅓ cup Parmesan cheese

Cut the crust off ten slices of white bread—regular, not thin.

Flatten the slices so thin you worry about them.

Butter the bread heavily. Slather away. Don't be mingy. By the way, the butter should be very soft. I guess I should have told you that earlier.

Spread the bread lightly with sour cream. I usually reason that if a little sour cream is good, a lot of sour cream is better, and sometimes I am sorry because this can lead to things falling apart, though not necessarily your life.

Smear a tablespoon or so of the mixture on each bread slice. Hey, I also forgot to tell you about the mixture. Sauté mushrooms, chopped chives, and scallions in 3 tablespoons of butter. Cooks who are goody-goodies prepare this beforehand.

Roll each piece of bread as if you were rolling up a poster of The Last Supper.

Dab some more butter on each roll. Why not?

Sprinkle with Parmesan cheese.

Put rolls in a 375-degree oven for 30 minutes or until they look like something you may want to eat.

When still hot, cut each roll into three pieces. It's not easy. You might want to hire a sushi chef or lumberjack for this part. On the other hand, how much do you care about what they look like?

Serve with chocolate turtles from the candy dish.

PATRICIA MARX is a staff writer for the *New Yorker,* a former writer for *Saturday Night Live,* and the first woman elected to the Harvard Lampoon. Her most recent book is *Let's Be Less Stupid: An Attempt to Maintain My Mental Faculties.* She teaches at Columbia, Stony Brook, and the 92nd Street Y. She received a 2015 Guggenheim Fellowship. She can take a baked potato out of the oven with her bare hand.

SHARON OLDS
EARLY IDEAS ABOUT MEALS

In the beginning was the Milk, and the Milk was with Mom, and the Milk was Mom. (There was, from the beginning, a shocking magic about food.)

When I was a child I believed that it was important to try to believe (and God could see what you thought!) that the scarily dry, the aggressively moisture-absorbent rounds of The Host were actually Jesus' flesh from 1,949 years before. The red wine, and the Death-Valley, saliva-absorbing wafers, were blood (the blood of a sacred child we had murdered) and flesh (His tissue, nerves, muscles, eyes, fat.)

And who had transmogrified His living blood (from the year 33 C.E.) into the wine served at the rail (or vice versa)? And how much more mysterious was that than my baby brother, when I was two, putting his mouth to our mother's breast and gulping?! "He thinks there's milk in there," my big sister reported with gentle pitying mockery. O there *is*, I thought, there *is*.

The first recipe I encountered was in a child's cookbook; it was for "Candle Salad." Painstakingly thorough directions led you to put a ring of canned pineapple on a plate, stick the top half of a banana down into the pineapple circle, and balance a maraschino cherry on top.

I was enthralled. It was as if I was there at the invention of metaphor. Banana = candle! Cherry = fire! And after wine = blood, it was easy, and it was *fun*.

My other memory of early ideas about meals was not a recipe but the concept of a menu for a meal. When the icebox (it was a refrigerator but we called it the icebox) was crowded with little saved portions of leftovers, my father liked to cut up a couple of months from the calendar, producing two sets of numbers from 1 to 30, and put May's days into his hat, and a June day in front of each of 30 dishes of old food, and what you drew from his hat you ate. He liked it if it was a food you hated. When it was Calendar Lunch, it was Calendar Lunch.

One final memory: I was 13 or 14, and noticed that I had a few friends—some from Girl Scout Camp, one from Berkeley Community Players (amateur actors), maybe one or two from Jr. High—I decided to "give a luncheon"; my idea, in 1956 or so, in my mother's house, of a rite of passage into adult femalehood. I had heard of Perle Mesta, I had the idea women could with some dignity be hostesses. So I found a recipe for "bridge sandwiches." I liked slicing a loaf of bread horizontally into three layers, spreading the fillings like frosting, then cutting the individual cross-sections—it pleased my brain in some primitive architectural/geometrical way. And I bought a Bundt pan and made an applesauce walnut spice cake with lemon frosting.

Howl would not come out for two years, across the Bay in San Francisco (Allen Ginsberg was writing some of it, I since learned, at the Berkeley Public Library). I had never considered the possibility of not wearing make-up, or not smoking cigarettes as soon as you were allowed to (15), or not growing up and giving luncheons!

I think it went all right. My mother had never cooked desserts, so I was interested in baking—it could become my own angle on the enterprise—pineapple upside-down cake, cheesecake with sour-cream frosting, chocolate roll (what's more thrilling than tilting it on its trampoline of waxed paper and feeling the curl of the wave begin?).

Let us pass gently from 1956 to 2015—some years of Julia Childs' "Daube de Boeuf en Gelée Jacques Pepin" in there—what did I cook, for myself, tonight?

Hot Cheddar with Contents

walnuts
raw cranberries
green olives (pitted)
fennel seeds
slices of Heluva Good! (or other)
   sharp cheddar cheese
a couple cloves of garlic, peeled
   and quartered or eighthed

Put a mixture of the nuts, fruits, and seeds, along with olives in a bowl. On top, the slices of Heluva cheese. Over that, the garlic. Pop in toaster oven. Outside, midsummer crickets and song sparrows and crows, and the oak (duir) moon (the Celtic goddess calendar I get from Luna Press)—("Her bird is the wren; her color, black; her healing powers cleanse and strengthen").

I'll often be eating one of these mongrel taste-bud-exciters while I'm reading—one world going on in my head, while a subterranean journey with milestones and turnstiles is happening in my mouth. Licorice! Walnut (toasty outside! Inside, meaty in its clean way), garlic (so sexual, sharp, penetrating, paradoxical, almost sweet), olives (one of the perfect foods, an Eden food). And cheese, informed with mammal grease and protein, taking me back to my first experience with the essential deliciousness of nourishment on earth.

SHARON OLDS has published 12 collections of poetry, including *Satan Says* (1980), *The Dead and The Living* (1984), *The Wellspring* (1996), and *Stag's Leap* (2013), which won both the Pulitzer and T.S. Eliot Prizes. Olds was New York State Poet Laureate 1998–2000 and currently teaches poetry workshops at the Graduate Program in Creative Writing at New York University.

MARINA ABRAMOVIĆ
SELECTIONS FROM <u>SPIRIT</u> <u>COOKING</u>
with ESSENTIAL APHRODISIAC RECIPES

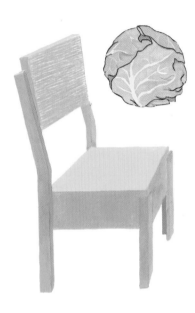

pain

in time of doubt
keep a small meteorite
stone
in your mouth

**to be consumed on a
solar eclipse**

take 13 leaves of uncut
green cabbage with
13,000 grams of jealousy
steam for a long time in a
deep iron pot
until all the water
evaporates
eat just before attack

essence drink

mix fresh breast milk
with
fresh sperm milk
drink on earthquake nights

fire food

on top of a volcano
open your mouth
wait until your tongue
becomes flame
close your mouth
take a deep breath

MARINA ABRAMOVIĆ has pioneered performance art since the beginning of her career in Belgrade during the early 1970s, creating some of the form's most important early works. The body has always been both her subject and medium. In 2010, Abramović had her first major U.S. retrospective and simultaneously performed for over 700 hours in "The Artist is Present" at the Museum of Modern Art in New York. She also founded the Marina Abramović Institute (MAI), a platform for immaterial and long durational work to create new possibilities for collaboration among thinkers of all fields.

HENRY ALFORD
SUMMER RECIPES

Sun-Dried Tomatoes

8 tomatoes
6 cups olive oil

Unscrew a 100-watt lightbulb while it is still gorgeously warm. With a rubbing motion, thrill the skins of the tomatoes until they start to pucker and tumesce. Uncork the oil; drizzle onto tomatoes until lubricious.

Skinny-Dipping at Dusk

8 cups water
25 pounds cocoa

Store the water in a cool place, allowing it to bio-ripen for a period lasting months or even years. Meanwhile, fill your largest roasting pan with cocoa. Roll in cocoa.

Gone Fishin'

1 telephone
1 couch

Unplug the telephone and assume a position on your couch which suggests an odalisque or any late-career Ingres portrait. Should people or problems present themselves, bite into a nougatty chocolate and say teasingly,

"I can't help you. I'm very Ingres-y with you." Let the slipcovers puddle around you like a light vinaigrette.

Summery Chinese Toboggan Salad

1 can bamboo shoots
½ cup sesame oil
4 stalks celery, chopped
juice and zest of 3 lemons
1 wooden toboggan

Put the toboggan in a food processor and pulse for ten seconds on Eviscerate. Remove the splinters from the processor and toss with other ingredients. Arrange on a plate with your bare hands, letting your fingers burrow into the mixture as they do when encountering the rich loam of the earth. Strike your gong.

August Romance

2 cups high-quality vinegar

10 toffee caramels

Unsheath the caramels laughingly, unconcerned of outcome. Fork-prick to soften. Using the soft pads of your thumb and index finger to palpate the caramels, tease them into the vinegar, saying, "Mummy knows what's best." Put the whole concoction away someplace dark. Have a glass of Prosecco with a friend, displaying blitheness and a tendency, when food has been dropped on the floor, to plop it back onto your plate with a soulful, sensuous expression.

Can you leave the vinegar alone for between three days and three weeks? Try to, darling—what you're doing here is tempering yourself as well as the candy. Enjoy this. Because when you return to the vinegar the caramels will be gone.

HENRY ALFORD writes for *The New York Times,* and is the author of five books, including, most recently, *Would It Kill You to Stop Doing That: A Modern Guide to Manners.*

HEIDI JULAVITS
RHUBARB

Very little edible grows in my Maine yard. I do not garden, cannot garden. My thumb conveys the touch of death to all plants except monkshood, which is poisonous, and since I failed to kill it, now it might someday kill me.

There exist non-poisonous plants that spontaneously grow in this climate without tending. Sometimes one of these plants appears in my yard. Chives grew once. Mint grew. I hoped other things might grow. Once, before we bought our house, my husband and I rented a house with rhubarb growing behind the barn. The house was located at the end of a very long peninsula. We often found ourselves craving food at hours we could not buy it, and besides, the nearest general store sold 50s-era cooking gelatin and flashlight batteries and little else. We discovered the rhubarb patch in a desperate moment, cooked down the stalks with sugar and poured cream over it, and called it dessert.

I am hoping that rhubarb might someday materialize in my current yard; like the chives and the mint, it will one day simply emerge from the ground, and as a result I can disappear into my yard and reappear with a meal. However, I was told by a local that rhubarb either comes with your property or it doesn't. We tried to buck the rhubarb zoning laws by attempting an illegal transplant: we carried some rhubarb from my neighbor's yard and put it in ours, hoping it would thrive. It did not.

Still, I have a facility with rhubarb (cooking it, I mean), even if I have to buy it or wait to receive it as a gift from a person with a native patch. I got to know it during more ingenious times. Rhubarb, even if you're eating it for dessert, should be really tart. It should practically cause canker sores on contact, causing your mouth a flooding pain. It should be like the ocean when you jump in, so cold you nearly hyperventilate.

Rhubarb Compote

4 stalks rhubarb (roughly 2-3 cups)
1 tablespoon or so sugar (more to
   taste, but don't overdo it)
juice from half a lemon
a splash of vanilla extract

Cut the rhubarb into chunks. Put in a pan with all other ingredients and heat. The rhubarb will give off lots of water eventually and turn pretty soupy. Stop cooking before all the pieces totally dissolve. Serve it hot with cold cream poured over it, or with oatmeal in the morning, or with a warm popover. As a condiment—on scones, for example—it's a variation on lemon curd, tart and a little sweet.

HEIDI JULAVITS is the author of four critically acclaimed novels, *The Vanishers, The Uses of Enchantment, The Effect of Living Backwards,* and *The Mineral Palace*, and, most recently, *The Folded Clock: A Diary.* She coedited, with Sheila Heti and Leanne Shapton, the bestselling *Women in Clothes.* A founding editor of *The Believer* magazine, Julavits teaches at Columbia University. She lives in Manhattan and Maine with her husband, Ben Marcus, and their two children.

SANFORD BIGGERS
RED TURN UP

I grew up in the 70s and 80s, in the Los Angeles neighborhood of View Park, a black, middle-class enclave that was too "hood" for my white friends and too "bougie" for my black friends. The homes were mid-century modern gems with three-car garages, front and back yards, swimming pools, recognizable Japanese and Hacienda-style flourishes, as well as panoramic views of downtown LA, the Hollywood sign, and the beach. Now the gentrifiers are Columbusing this "new" prime real estate, and blacks are decrying, "Why they always gotta take all of our shit?!"

Back then, one of my favorite summertime traditions was the neighborhood 4th of July BBQ. Each year it would rotate from house to house, giving the host a chance to show off a new car, pool, or home improvement, as well as a chance to proclaim the new

jam of the summer—think Earth Wind & Fire's "Boogie Wonderland," Taste of Honey's "Boogie Oogie Oogie," or all of Stevie Wonder's *Songs in the Key of Life*.

Of course, in addition to music, there was food. Everyone always shared their very best: homemade briskets, BBQ ribs, pork and beans, potato salads, greens, peach cobblers, pineapple upside down cakes. An often-overlooked staple was red drink. Throughout my childhood, I saw red drinks range from red Kool-Aid to mysterious home concoctions, but the essential element was always the color itself. And yes, the flavor is red, not cherry as frequently mistaken.

Red drinks are the official libations of soul cooking. As with many things African American, the roots of this drink can be traced back to Africa and/or the Caribbean, to drinks such as bissap or sorrel. Here, I'd like to offer you my artisanal update of that Soul food classic. Think of it as something tasty to lessen the bitter taste of consistent, systematic oppression, unequal distribution of wealth and resources, aggressive gentrification, and long-term disenfranchisement throughout U.S. history.

Red Drink Turn-up
(aka Red Turnup)

1 ½ ounces quality mezcal (Ilegal, Del Maguey, or similar is suggested)
1 cup cubed watermelon
cilantro—1 sprig for muddling, 1 sprig for garnish
freshly ground salt and chili mixture for glass rim
lime wedge
¾ cups of ice
agave to taste (optional)

Mix salt and chili powder in a bowl, pour onto a saucer. Rub the rim of an old fashioned glass with a wedge of lime. Dip rim of glass into the salt mixture until rim is lightly dusted.

Muddle one sprig of cilantro inside the glass and set aside. Place the watermelon and mezcal into a blender. Blend until watermelon purées. Add ¾ cup of ice into the glass. Pour watermelon mezcal mixture over the ice. Add a sprig of cilantro for garnish. Makes one cocktail.

SANFORD BIGGERS is a visual artist producing paintings, sculptures, immersive installations, and video. Biggers also creates multimedia musical performances with his collective Moon Medicin. He has shown his work in venues worldwide including Tate Britain, Tate Modern, the Whitney Museum, Studio Museum in Harlem, and the Yerba Buena Center for the Arts, and his works are included in the collections of the Museum of Modern Art, Walker Art Center, Whitney Museum, Brooklyn Museum and Bronx Museum. Born and raised in LA, Biggers currently lives and works in NYC, where he is Associate Professor at Columbia University's Visual Arts program.

LIZA LOU
FEMINIST POPCORN

My mother told me and my sister that we should never learn to cook.

"Be careful of what you get good at, because you'll end up having to do it," my mom told us. She often delivered pithy life instructions while we waited for dinner.

After our father flew the coop and offered no child support, my mom learned to drive a car. She put herself through school, too, so she could make a better life for us with no help from anyone. She did everything, but one thing she stopped doing with joy was cooking.

But, we still popped lots of popcorn. And we had lots of poppers. We had the popcorn pumper that looked like an upright torpedo and the hot air popper that shot popcorn out of what looked like a public hair dryer. We also had the As-Seen-On-TV version where we watched the popcorn explode in an amber plastic dome and when it was done popping, flipped it over and ate it straight out of the plastic. When microwave, fat-free popcorn came along, at first we thought we'd hit prairie gold, but my sister and I were not skilled with heat. The bag would get scorched and there were always lots of charcoal kernels, which we would eat.

The Iroquois are said to have believed that there is a soul living inside every kernel of popcorn, and maybe they were right, maybe there is a soul living inside absolutely everything, just waiting for the right amount of distress and friction to make it transform into something else.

Feminist Popcorn

¾ cup popcorn kernels
a lug of canola oil
25 grams butter
sea salt to taste

Use a large pot with a glass lid. Keep the lid very slightly ajar.

Measure out ¾ cups of kernels. Set aside.

Pour just enough canola oil to cover the bottom of the pot. Add 3 kernels of popcorn and turn on high heat. When the 3 kernels of corn have popped, your oil is ready—quickly add the rest of the popcorn, shaking the pan so that kernels are spread evenly. Now shake the pot back and forth, back and forth. The secret is to keep shaking the pot without stopping.

When you can count to three and nothing pops in between, immediately remove from heat and pour into large bowl.

If you're feeling blood thirsty, melt butter in the now-empty pot, add to taste.

Add sea salt to taste.

LIZA LOU is an artist who first gained attention with her room sized sculpture, *Kitchen,* now in the Whitney Museum's permanent collection. This groundbreaking work introduced glass beads as Lou's primary art material, and established many of the social and political themes—women's issues, social justice, endurance—that underscore her practice today. Lou has exhibited in major museums around the world, including The Metropolitan Museum of Art, the Victoria and Albert Museum, and the Smithsonian Institution of American Art. She is a recipient of a MacArthur Foundation Fellowship, and lives and works in Los Angeles and South Africa.

ED PARK
CRACKERS WITH CHEESE & LEFTOVERS

Why settle for plain crackers when you can also apply a small wedge of cheese to it? The benefits can be enormous, and it requires minimal effort.

Crackers with Cheese

crackers (1–80)
cheese, any kind (one chunk)

You'll also need these non-edible devices:

1 plate
1 knife

You'll also need:

1 mouth
1 digestive system

Optional:

1 napkin (for crumbs)
1 glass (for beverage)
1 beverage (water, e.g.)

Open the box of crackers and puncture the plastic wrapping.

Unwrap the chunk of cheese and cut a thin wedge from it. Make sure it's not wider or longer than the crackers.

If the cheese has a spot of mold, you can throw out the whole thing, or just pare away the bad bit. If you throw it away, you need to go out and buy more cheese, so—think about it.

Place the wedge on cracker, place the entire thing into mouth, chew, and swallow.

Repeat til satisfied. (Typical time: 15 minutes–2 hours.)

Leftovers

For this recipe, you'll need:

1 leftovers from dinner
1 portion of baguette
1 microwave oven

(Important note: For baguette, you can substitute any sort of loaf bread, or a bagel, and possibly a knish.)

You'll also need:

1 plate

And you'll probably need:

1 fork or
1 spoon

And also:

1 hand

And:

1 mouth
1 digestive system

What you do:

Heat up the leftovers on a plate, using your microwave. Time varies: 1 minute, sometimes 2, occasionally more. Best to set the oven on "high."

Serve. Mop juices with bread.

Afterward, place plate in sink and think about washing it. (Contemplation should last from 1 hour up to 2 days.)

ED PARK is the creator of the popular Facebook meme "Hall and Joyce Carol Oates." He is the author of the novel *Personal Days*, a founding editor of *The Believer,* and Executive Editor at Penguin Press. He lives and eats in Manhattan.

SWEETS

DANIYAL MUEENUDDIN
MRS. ISKIAN'S CHEESECAKE

My maternal grandfather, Roland Louis Thompson, brought up on a hard-scrabble 80-acre farm in Wisconsin's driftless country, father dying early, eldest of 11 children (none of whom amounted to "a hill of beans" other than him)—put himself through college at UW-Madison back in the early 20th century, then med school, stoking furnaces, according to my mother's chased and chiseled story, one of her many stories

about the family past. In the early 1920s, he married Dagney Buseth, a Norwegian girl with a somewhat un-Norwegian air—she is described as going to a party with him wearing long silk gloves to her elbows, removing them to drink punch, and forgetting them on the settee when they next rose to dance—a blithe forgetfulness utterly cool and deliciously attractive to the boy from Elroy, Wisconsin. On his graduation, they drove in a Model T Ford cross country, on roads that then were little better than wagon trails, to the land of opportunity, Los Angeles, California. Over the years he had great success there as a surgeon and GP, treating high and low, buying lots of property back home in Elroy, always still the boy from Elroy.

The invalid widowed Mrs. Iskian, who had no money at all, needed expensive treatments and regular house calls from her doctor, one Roland Louis Thompson. He was greatly addicted to the TV show "Gunsmoke"—found in Mrs. I a fellow aficionado—and so would go over of an afternoon to her little house, watch *Gunsmoke*, render her a free consultation, and be paid in cheesecake; hers was superlative, and he had a great tooth for this delicacy. Though he would gently suggest that she might give him the recipe—in between bites,

and while sipping a cup of hot coffee and watching *Gunsmoke* on her black-and-white set, all the time rocking in a rocking chair with such absorption that he would rock himself right across the living room and have to pick up the chair and shimmy it back nearer to the set—though he often made this suggestion, the recipe was not forthcoming, and so the besotted man found it necessary often to visit the Widow Iskian. Upon her death, at an advanced age, and of some painless lapse in her constitution, the recipe was found addressed to him in her bedside table. I give it below, exactly as my mother in turn gave it to me. I have never made it, but certainly mean to, though it will never be as delicious as when my mother served it to me, driving home a bowl of her chili, so many times over so many years.

Mrs. Iskian's Cheesecake Recipe
(for RLT, drawer next to her bed)

Crust:

1 teaspoon cinnamon
16 graham crackers rolled into
    crumbs (2 cups)
¼ cup light brown sugar
5 tablespoons butter, soft

Filling:

1 large package cream cheese
    (8 ounces) and 1 small package
    (3 ounces)
1 small container sour cream (8
    ounces)

3 large eggs, add slowly as you
    beat
⅔ cup sugar
1 teaspoon vanilla
1 tablespoon lemon juice

Topping:

1 cup sour cream
3 tablespoons sugar
1 teaspoon vanilla
zest of one small lemon, or to taste

Mix crust ingredients well with hands and wooden spoon, press neatly into pie tin and chill.

Combine ingredients for cheesecake, beat til light and frothy.

Pour into firmly chilled crust.

Bake 35 minutes at preheated 375-degree oven.

COOL!

Mix ingredients for topping well and pour over cooled filling.

Bake 10 minutes at 350.

DANIYAL MUEENUDDIN was brought up in Lahore, Pakistan and Elroy, Wisconsin. He is the author of a short story collection *In Other Rooms, Other Wonders,* which won The Story Prize, was a *New York Times* bestseller, and has been translated into 20 languages. His new novel, *Kristal,* is partly set in Elroy, Wisconsin. He continues to own and to farm land in Wisconsin that belonged to his grandfather.

CHRISTINE SCHUTT
Fancy Cake

Barbara Froemming Dreazy's Famous French Chocolate Cake and Icing, a special occasion cake from the Junior League, is a noisy, dangerous, effortful undertaking, which when done right produces a sublimely light, yet moist, cake. The airy icing is violently made with a hand-mixer applied to the contents of a metal bowl held in a bigger bowl full of ice—so much for the gracious life, circa 1959. My mother and Barbara Froemming Dreazy were friends then, which explains why my mother, who was never comfortable in clubs, made the famous French cake in the first place. She liked Barbara. "She makes me stand on my toes," Mother said, "but in a cheerful way."

She springs from around the corner and into our kitchen in the memory I have of her: Barbara Froemming Dreazy, a foxy-colored woman, freckled and quick; hoarse voice, rapid speech—barbed asides from Barbara that I don't understand. Childless (by choice?), Barbara Froemming Dreazy does not appear to like children, and she whisks past me to Mother, crimping foil around the cake plate. "Done!"

"You didn't!"

"I did!"

"Sally!" she enthuses and embraces my mother, who is much taller than Mrs. Dreazy, so that she makes herself smaller and hunkers close.

Mother grew so proficient in the making of Barbara Froemming Dreazy's famous cake as to surpass the original baker's version—at least that's what Mother said she, Barbara Froemming Dreazy, had said.

Mother said, "Can you believe it? And Barbara speaks French."

Mother spoke no other languages, and by her own admission did poorly in Latin. Barbara Froemming Dreazy was a graduate of Smith; my mother didn't finish college. "I had you instead," she liked to say, "but it didn't keep me out of the smart set column."

Few doors stayed closed to my mother when she knocked.

I associate this cake with membership in the smart set, of which Barbara Froemming Dreazy was once president, and my mother, for a time, a member. To make the famous French cake is to renew dues, wear cable-knit sweaters and Belgian flats.

French Chocolate Cake

This cake has a velvety texture and is very, very moist. Don't worry if it falls a bit.

½ cup cocoa (instant)
¾ cup boiling water
1 cup sour cream
½ teaspoon baking soda
½ cup butter
1 cup sugar
2 cups cake flour measured after 2
    siftings
3 egg whites, beaten stiff
1 teaspoon vanilla

Preheat oven to 300 degrees. Mix together cocoa and water and combine with baking soda dissolved in sour cream. Cream butter with sugar using a hand or stand mixer. To the butter and sugar alternately add in the sifted flour and cocoa mixture. Beat until fluffy. Fold in egg whites and vanilla. Pour batter into greased 9 x 13-inch pan and bake for 50 minutes. Do not remove from pan. Ice with the following to-die-for whipped chocolate frosting.

Ice Chocolate Frosting

1 egg
1 cup powdered sugar
¼ cup milk
dash of vanilla
2 squares melted bitter
    (unsweetened) chocolate
½ pound butter

Melt the chocolate squares and butter in a pan and set aside, allowing to cool. Mix the egg, sugar, milk, and vanilla in a bowl (preferably metal) and place it in a larger bowl filled with ice cubes. Add the melted ingredients to the mixture and beat at high speed until the frosting turns a light color and the texture is firm.

CHRISTINE SCHUTT is the author of two short story collections and three novels. Her first novel, *Florida,* was a National Book Award finalist; her second novel, *All Souls,* a finalist for the 2009 Pulitzer Prize. A third novel, *Prosperous Friends,* was noted in *The New Yorker* as one of the best books of 2012. Among other honors, Schutt has twice won the O. Henry Short Story Prize. She is the recipient of the New York Foundation of the Arts and Guggenheim Fellowships. Schutt lives and teaches in New York.

JULIE HEFFERNAN
CAKE WITH CARROTS

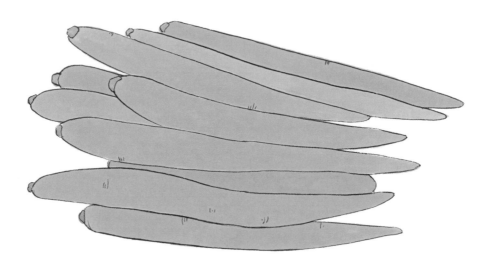

When I was five, my family moved to California from Peoria. This was still the California of ranches, orange trees, and burgeoning suburbs—Coors Beer was the drug of choice, not yet mescaline or LSD. We lived on an artery of the main drag, in one of those horrible houses they now describe as "midcentury modern." There was a strip mall on the corner; housewives with cocktails in hand stepped off curbs to talk to neighbors. *Back to Eden* hadn't yet been published and "The Summer of Love" was still years away.

My mother was a typical stay-at-home mom who cooked every night and made Whip'n Chill for dessert. So when an old Irish aunt shared her memory of making carrot cake from surplus canned carrots after WWII, I was intrigued. I knew you could make apple pie crust using Ritz crackers, but cake with carrots?

One Saturday afternoon, my best friend Kim came over and we decided to give it a try. We emptied all of the eggs in the refrigerator into a large bowl, and then added some other things you might need for chocolate chip cookies since we could find that recipe on the back of the Toll House wrapper. If the batter seemed too dry, we added more Wesson oil and then more grated carrots. Cinnamon seemed right too, so we added it in, tossing it in the oven at the usual 350 degrees. Despite all our guesswork and improvisations, the cake came out golden brown and tasting fantastic.

Later that year, in 5th grade at St. Clements Catholic School, our homework for science class was to bake something and bring it in to present to the class. Of course I brought in my carrot cake, but Danny Lyon—whom I had a crush on because he seemed like a renegade—was the only one with enough imagination to give it a try; everyone else was horrified by the idea of a cake with vegetables in it. Which, in the end, was fine: I brought the leftovers home, ate it myself, and have been baking and eating it ever since.

Carrot Cake

- 4 extra-large or 5 large eggs
- 1 cup canola oil
- 1 cup raw sugar
- 2 cups unbleached flour
- 3 tablespoons cinnamon
- 1 teaspoon salt
- 2 teaspoons baking soda
- 2 cups grated carrots
- 1 cup walnuts
- 1 cup chocolate chips (optional)

Mix all ingredients together, adding carrots, walnuts and chocolate chips last. Bake at 350 in an 8 x 12-inch greased pan for about 45 minutes, or until you can really smell the cake and a knife inserted comes out clean.

JULIE HEFFERNAN is a Professor of Fine Arts at Montclair State University in New Jersey. She received her MFA at Yale School of Art in 1985. Currently, she is represented by PPOW Gallery in New York City, Catharine Clark Gallery in San Francisco, CA, and Mark Moore Gallery in Los Angeles, CA.

AÏDA RUILOVA
STRANGER IN MY HOUSE

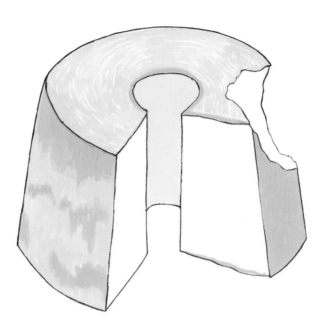

We met at night under a tree in the small church graveyard next door to my house. His dirt bike was leaning on the ground beside him, and he threw his cigarette down as he saw me approaching. He was 14 and I was 13. I swung my arms up around his neck and we started kissing.

Chris was gangly and tall, and looking into his eyes felt like drowning in secrets. He and his three brothers were adopted by a Christian preacher and all had been in and out of juvie for various petty crimes. The one time I rode by his house, I remember seeing the brothers hovering in a front yard littered with old burnt out car parts and trash, their deep set dark brown eyes penetrating through all the trash, straight into my heart.

We were lying on the ground as he ran his fingers down the center of my torso, when suddenly his voice made me freeze. "Do you wanna know where my fingers have been?" he said in a deep, affected voice. I nodded and giggled nervously, thinking it would bring his normal voice back. But his voice only got lower, worse, and he began singing, "There's a stranger in my house...and I don't know who he is...but he's trying to steal my..." I pulled away quickly.

He sat up. "I'm hungry," he announced. His normal voice was back. We snuck into my house, and I was searching the fridge when I heard the sound of him eating. He had already found the Angel Food Cake and ripped out a piece, leaving an impression where the cake was missing.

Angel Food Cake

18 egg whites
2 teaspoons cream of tartar
1 pinch salt
1 ½ cups white sugar
1 cup cake flour
½ cup confectioners' sugar
1 teaspoon vanilla extract

Preheat oven to 350. Sift cake flour and confectioner's sugar together and set aside.

In a large bowl, whip egg whites with a pinch of salt until foamy. Add cream of tartar and continue beating until soft peaks form.

Gradually add sugar while beating, and continue to beat until very stiff. Add vanilla.

Quickly fold in flour mixture. Pour into a 10-inch tube pan.

Bake at 350 for 45 minutes.

AÏDA RUILOVA's videos combine classical cinematic devices with a distinctively low-tech sensibility, quick cuts, and rhythmic, jarring soundtracks to create works that exist in the space between sound and image. Her work has been shown in numerous galleries, museums, and multiple international art biennials, and she was nominated for the Hugo Boss Prize in 2006.

MANIL SURI
TEMPTED BY THE FRUIT

Before puberty, before the swells and curves of the human body became such an obsession, I began to notice fruit: coconuts swaying with their palms in tropical breezes from the Arabian Sea, egg-shaped sapodillas nestling slyly in the folds of trees, the flash of the occasional golden guava hanging out of reach.

Mumbai, or Bombay as it was called then, was a sea of buildings, so it was always a thrill to come upon a tree full of fruit. There were three in my neighborhood, and every weekend I went on a fruit-sighting tour. Windy days were the best, because then there would be offerings waiting when I rooted around at their bases. What I really craved, though, were the mangoes dangling in clusters from the branches of the tree that spread out over our school compound. I would stand underneath during lunch recess, enthralled by their green smooth-

skinned voluptuousness, hoping for one to fall.

Once there was a hot April week without wind. The mangoes hung heavy and motionless above me; the bushes around the base had long ago been picked clean. By Friday, the provocation became too much. I found myself picking up a round stone and hurling it at one of the clusters. It must have been beginner's luck, because I hit the cluster dead on. Stems swung in the air, fruit shook, and not one but two mangoes fell to earth. They were large ones too, not the puny specimens that dropped in the wind. I took bites of raw mango that day until my teeth turned sour. I was hooked—after that, I started lobbing stones at fruit trees whenever nobody was around.

But this new activity didn't last long. It turned out there were always witnesses around—moreover, they were rarely amused. A broken window or two quickly checked my slide into complete delinquency. I learnt to restrain my hunting impulses, and contented myself with ogling and gathering.

At the age of 20, I came to Pittsburgh to study, and my quest for fruit remained as passionate in the New World. I found fulfillment at the supermarket: blueberries and blackberries and impossibly red raspberries (all I had seen in Bombay were strawberries). Even pears came in startling gold and red varieties. My housemates refused to go shopping with me because of all the time I spent mesmerized in the fruit section. Still, I missed the mangoes hanging over the streets of Bombay. The wild apple tree I stumbled upon in my neighborhood park couldn't compare. Not that I dared throw stones at its discolored fruit anyway—in this orderly land, I could imagine the shocked looks that would elicit.

The Washington, DC area where I moved to take up a university position proved to be a better place for finding fruit. Black stains on the sidewalk turned out to be mulberries. Over the July 4th weekend, I found scores of wild raspberries lining my bicycle trail. In autumn, the crabapple trees in my neighborhood were all suddenly ablaze with fruit. But, I still didn't have my green card—could I be deported for sampling some in plain view of the street?

The toughest challenge to my "no plucking" code of conduct came some years later at Thomas Jefferson's plantation in Monticello. There were rolling slopes covered with fruit trees—peaches, plums, apricots, and nectarines were all in season. One section had plantings of raspberries and gooseberries and figs, another had vines brimming with grapes. The problem was there was nothing on the ground—the orchards were so pristinely maintained that my rightful share of fallen fruit had been swept away. I had to remind myself of my recent American naturalization—if I stole from one of the founding fathers, what would my new countrymen think of me?

Perhaps Jefferson fueled the desire to have my own orchard once I moved into a house. It seemed to be the natural culmination of my passion—the fruit I sought, brought forth from my own land, with my own hands. The house already had a grape arbor, and even though the yard was small, in went two rows of blackberry bushes, a red currant bush, a fig tree, and a quince. Somehow, there was still space left over to squeeze in a miniature sour cherry tree, another fig, and a dwarf plum. The problems arose quite quickly. Birds ate the cherries, and the grapes were beset by black rot. The quinces dried and fell off, excessive rain swelled up the figs and turned them to mush. Wasps and mosquitoes descended in droves, attacking not just the berries and plums, but anyone who dared venture into the garden. Since the idea of cutting down the fruit trees was too abhorrent, there was only one thing to do—sell the house and move to another one. Needless to say, the new garden has remained strictly fruit-free.

Nowadays, I indulge my cravings in a more pre-packaged way—I go to a "pick your own" farm. Updates arrive conveniently by e-mail all summer, telling me what's ripe in the fields or the trees each week. It's a little like shooting fish in a barrel, of course—the thrill of the chase is gone. But the strawberries are vibrantly red against their beds, the plums dark and shapely in their trees, the apples smooth and blemish-free.

Still, just gathering isn't enough; I also need to hunt. For this, I drive to Virginia in September and take the exit for Great Falls. Parking well before the falls, I cross the road to a trail that leads into the woods. The leaves have just begun to turn and there is already a chill in the air. I walk until I sense the river is near.

That's when the thickets begin to emerge—the pawpaw trees that grow all along the banks of the Potomac. But none of them have fruit. Could someone have beaten me to the hunt, stripped the branches clean? I decide to leave the path—the ground is soft beneath my boots, the foliage closes behind me.

I am surrounded by trees, with the river barely audible, when I spot the cluster of pawpaws above me. They look just like mangoes, green and oval—though they taste different, I know they will be similarly yellow inside. I find a stone and the muscles in my arm tense reflexively. For an instant the miles and years fade away—I am back in Bombay under my school tree. The target sharpens in focus, the air clears, and with a familiar ripple through my shoulder, the stone flies free.

$\longrightarrow$

Mango-Blueberry Pie

9-inch uncooked deep dish pie
   crust (frozen, store bought is fine)
   in a pie pan
2 large eggs, lightly beaten
2 tablespoons flour
⅔ cup granulated sugar
⅓ cup melted butter
2 large (or 3 small) ripe mangoes
   (see note below), flesh cut into
   chunks
1 cup blueberries

I've often made the wonderful (and wonderfully simple) peach pie from *The Joy of Cooking*. One day, I only had two peaches, so I substituted a mango for the rest—after all, the two fruits are similar in consistency and color. The result was delicious—the mango part tasted even better than the peach. So I started making it with all mango—until the day came when I didn't have enough mango. I decided to throw in a cup of blueberries to make up the difference—and voilà, this recipe was born. The combination of mango and blueberry has a complex flavor and aroma, which is unexpected given the simplicity of the recipe. The pie is good with vanilla ice cream or whipped cream, but I prefer to splash it with unsweetened heavy cream, straight from the carton.

Preheat oven to 400. Mix together eggs, butter, flour, and sugar. Spread mango chunks in pie crust and top with blueberries. Pour egg mixture on top. Place pie pan on cookie sheet and bake 15 minutes. Then reduce heat to 300 and bake for 50 minutes more. Cool completely before serving.

Note: Store-bought mangoes can often be unripe. Be sure to ripen on counter for a few days before using. The flesh should be soft, not crisp, and should taste sweet.

MANIL SURI is a mathematics professor at the University of Maryland, Baltimore County, and is the author of the novels, *The Death of Vishnu, The Age of Shiva,* and *The City of Devi.* He is a contributing opinion writer for *The New York Times*. Suri lives with his partner in Silver Spring, MD in a house with a large yard, but not enough sun to cultivate fruit trees.

JESSICA STOLLER
MALE GAZE MACARONS

Male Gaze Macarons

3 egg whites
your best catcall
¼ cup refined sugar
1 pair high heels OR 2 pieces
   form-fitting clothing
1 ⅔ cups confectioners' sugar
a pinch of straight porn
1 cup finely ground almonds

Line a baking sheet with a silicone baking mat and preheat your oven to 285 degrees.

Add your best catcall: *Hey baby! SexXxXy!! Can I get your number? GOD BLESS YOU. Let me get some of that SUGAR!! Smile for me??*

Beat your egg whites in the bowl fitted with a whisk attachment until the egg whites can no longer ignore being harassed and foam in response.

Add pair of high heels OR 2 pieces of form fitting clothing. With rapt eyes, beat in refined sugar and continue mixing aggressively until egg whites are glossy, fluffy, and hold soft peaks for all to see.

Sift in confectioners sugar and ground almonds in a separate bowl and quickly fold almond mixture into the egg whites after about 30 strokes. If delusional, give a privileged pinch to make sure mixture is to your liking.

Spoon a small amount of batter into a plastic bag and cut off edge of bag so plastic hole is exposed, add a pinch of straight porn for unrealistic expectations.

Pipe dollop of mixture about 1 ½ inch in diameter onto prepared baking sheets. Let piped flat disks stand at room temp until hard, jaded skin forms.

Preheat oven to 285 degrees.

Bake macarons until set but not browned, about 10 minutes.

Let your disks cool completely before filling with unwanted stares and empty calories.

JESSICA STOLLER is a ceramicist best known for her elaborate porcelain sculptures that investigate ideas of consumption, desire, and idealized femininity. Stoller has exhibited her sculptures in the U.S. and abroad, and is a Pollock-Krasner and Peter S. Reed grantee. Born in 1981, Stoller is originally from Metro Detroit and currently lives and works in Brooklyn, New York. She is represented by PPOW Gallery.

TAVARES STRACHAN
SUNDAY DINNER IN THE BAHAMAS

Growing up in Nassau, Bahamas, my mother's side of the family—all 13 of my aunts, uncles, and dozens of cousins—would gather at my grandmother's house for Sunday dinner. Grammy lived in a lower middle class neighborhood in the center of the island, just a few miles from Bay Street and the cruise ships and the tourists bound for Paradise Island. But it was a part of the country that visitors would never see. Bus drivers, teachers, and shop workers lived in this warren of one-story cement homes painted teal, yellow, and pink, candy-colored hues that shimmered in the Caribbean sunlight.

Folks always began to arrive at her house in the early afternoon, and by the time the sun set, the street was lined with cars. The children would run around Grammy's small backyard, trampling the grass and playing tag around the bushes of bougainvillea and hibiscus. Inside the kitchen, my grandmother presided over my aunts as they heated up glistening platters of macaroni casserole, fried plantains in shallow pans of hot oil, and argued over how to cook the pork. In the front yard, my uncles grilled whole snappers, smoke billowing into the driveway, as they shit-talked and yelled at their kids to stay out of the street.

In my family, we did not eat formally. We didn't use linens or silver, and there was definitely no table on the island big enough to fit our whole clan. We ate standing or sitting wherever there was space, the food dished out on disposable plates with cups of Goombay punch or soda, gossip and laughter seasoning the meal.

As the sky darkened, the adults would pass around a gallon jug of sky juice, a dangerously delicious concoction of gin, fresh coconut water, and condensed milk. Eventually, my uncles would start a boisterous game of checkers or dominoes that would last until their kids were passed out and their wives were already halfway to the car, threatening to leave them behind, a container of leftovers tucked into their purses.

If you were very lucky, you ended one of those Sunday dinners with a sliver of my grandmother's coconut pie: a creamy yellow moon of a pie, flecked bronze in the heat of the oven, the custard laden with fresh, hand-grated coconut and rising from a butter crust.

For reasons I will never wholly understand but know better than to question, my grandmother made only two pies. One pie was exclusively for my grandfather, to be consumed at his leisure. The second pie was for everyone else. Needless to say, you rarely got firsts, let alone seconds. When you did get a slice, however, it was like winning the lottery.

Years later, in the tiny galley kitchen of my graduate school apartment in New Haven, I experienced such an urgent longing for this pie that I called my grandmother for the recipe. Usually my family is very secretive about recipes, but I was one of the first to leave for university so she thought I earned it. As per her instructions, I broke my supermarket coconut on the pavement in front of the apartment building, and grated the shards of white flesh down to nubs, just as she described.

When I finally took the pie out of the oven and set it to cool on the countertop, it hit me: *the whole pie was mine.* I was finally afforded the kingly status of my grandfather. I didn't have to share with my five brothers or any of my cousins. I could sit and eat this pie all night, if I wanted.

But I just couldn't bear to eat it alone. So I made a few calls, and soon enough, half a dozen of my new classmates filled my small apartment. They sat cross-legged on my floor and perched on the edge of my futon. Together we ate slices of pie on paper plates.

In recent years, my family has started to fracture, the get-togethers becoming fewer and far between. But whenever I eat this coconut pie, I picture us as we were, spilling out the seams of my grandparents' teal house.

Grammy's Coconut Pie

For the pastry:

2 cups all-purpose unbleached flour
1 teaspoon salt
1 8-ounce stick unsalted butter, cut into pieces
½–1 cup ice water

For the filling:

2 cups freshly grated coconut (see below for instructions)
4 egg yolks
1 can sweetened condensed milk
1 8-ounce stick unsalted butter, room temperature
1 teaspoon vanilla

To make the crust, combine dry ingredients. Cut in the butter with a fork until the mixture resembles coarse crumbs. Add ice water by the tablespoon until the mixture forms a ball, then wrap the dough in plastic wrap and refrigerate for at least one hour before rolling and placing in a pie pan.

For the grated coconut, first you need to break the coconut open. Go outside and throw the coconut on the pavement. If it doesn't break on the first go, try again until the coconut is in several pieces.

Then, using a butter knife, pry the white coconut flesh out of the broken shards. This will take some doing, and may seem cumbersome at first. Do not give up! Fresh coconut is the key ingredient to this pie.

Rinse the pieces of coconut to get rid of any debris.

Grate the pieces of coconut with a box grater, using the side with the finest holes. Try to grate each piece down to the nubs, taking care not to grate your fingertips.

Now you're ready to preheat your oven to 325. Beat egg yolks with vanilla until the mixture is fluffy. Then, using a wooden spoon, stir in butter, condensed milk, and vanilla. Fold in grated coconut until evenly distributed. Pour this mixture into the prepared crust and bake for 50 minutes, or until the top of the pie is golden.

TAVARES STRACHAN may be best known for his internationally celebrated piece, *The Distance Between What We Have and What We Want,* consisting of a 4.5-ton block of ice harvested in a river near Mount McKinley, Alaska. The ice was then sent via Federal Express to the Bahamas, where it was placed in a transparent refrigerated case and exhibited in Nassau. Over the past decade, Strachan's explorations have expanded to both outer space and deep sea, focusing on the human body's ability to acclimatize itself to these extreme environments. Born in Nassau, Bahamas, he lives and works in New York City.

FERNE JACOBS
THE WITCH'S RECIPE

Many years ago, while teaching in Anchorage, Alaska, I purchased an Inuit doll made by doll maker Rosalie Paniyak. I was fascinated by the doll's expression. She had a knowing look on her face and an enigmatic smile; to me she seemed so self-contained that it sometimes felt spooky. Because of this, I thought of her as a witch, and that is what I grew to call her. In those days, my artwork explored the symbol of a container (or cauldron) as a place to house the soul. So the first time I was asked to give a talk about my work as a visual artist, I decided to include a picture of the Witch. Before giving the talk, I imagined the following scene:

The Witch mixed her brew. Then, all of a sudden, she threw the brew into the air. I watched as it fell as snowflakes. Afterwards, she turned to look at me with a smile and said, "This is all I ever need. I eat the snow." I asked the Witch, "What happens if there are those who can't just eat the snow?" She answered that everyone can. When I asked again, she replied in an agitated manner, "In each of us is the ability to make the brew

from the fire; when you throw it into the air properly, it turns into snow and becomes food for the soul. Now leave me alone."

I didn't know what all of this meant until a friend of mine sent me a picture of a snowy landscape. He told me that he had been out walking after a snowstorm, photographing his footsteps in the snow. The next day, he took another walk where he had been before. He watched as a new snowfall filled his footprints.

Later, I watched the film *The Dead*, directed by John Huston and based on a short story by James Joyce. At the end, a couple goes back to their hotel room after attending a Christmas party, and the woman begins to cry. She tells her husband the story of a young man who risked his life to come see her when he was sick and had to trudge through the snow, and as a result, soon passed away. Her husband thinks that he is incapable of loving anyone so much. Then, gazing out the window, he sees that it is snowing all over Ireland, over the living and the dead.

When I had these experiences, I felt that I understood something about the cauldron and the snow. And so that is the Witch's "recipe," and it's simple in that there are only a few ingredients and instructions. But is it easy? I would say that all of life is in that cauldron, more complicated than we imagine.

Sugar-on-Snow

snow
maple syrup

If you want to sweeten the Witch's recipe, try this old, magical way to make candy using snow. To make it, heat maple syrup in a pan until it boils. Then, immediately pour it in strips over clean, packed snow, and watch as it transforms into thin, delicate sheets of maple taffy. Wrap around a popsicle stick or wind around a fork. Eat while watching the snow fill your footprints.

FERNE JACOBS is a fiber artist who creates sensuous sculptural baskets, forms, and wall hangings. Her work can be found in the permanent collections of museums including the Smithsonian American Art Museum in Washington, DC, the Metropolitan Museum of Art in New York, the Mint Museum in Charlotte, North Carolina, and the Contemporary Museum in Honolulu, Hawaii. Ferne Jacobs' honors include NEA Fellowships and a nomination to the American Craft Council College of Fellows. Born in Chicago, she lives and works in Los Angeles.

BHARATI MUKHERJEE
PAYESH

For middleclass Bengalis, food is love.

Growing up in Calcutta, I often attended elaborate Sunday lunches that my uncle would host for scores of relatives in his modest apartment. Through many gossipy hours in the kitchen, my female relatives chopped, diced, sliced, fried, braised, simmered. The menu usually included staggering varieties of appetizers, curried vegetable, fish and mutton entrées, sweet-sour palate refreshers and sweetmeats, and each cook took pride in preparing her specialty. The feast ended with several store-bought desserts: sweet, pink yoghurt, sandesh, cham-cham, syrup-soaked white rosogolla, brown pantua. And, with payesh, a creamy, comforting, home-made rice pudding.

Days after my 21st birthday, I left my hometown of Calcutta to study for a two-year MFA degree at The Writers' Workshop at the University of Iowa. My father's plan in sending me so far away from home was to give

himself enough time to select the Bengali Brahmin bridegroom worthiest of joining our family. His plan almost worked; he found his perfect groom, and the marital negotiations were completed by the time I was finishing my MFA degree. Then the unthinkable happened: I fell in love without my father's permission, and married the man of my choice.

I began to cook only after I married Clark. More accurately, for the first year of our marriage, I was the nervous "prep" assistant, tasked with taking out thick, bloody steaks from our third-hand refrigerator, and my husband the confident griller, pan-fryer, baker. In our Calcutta home, we had never eaten beef, and the barely-singed steak made me long for Bengali dishes with an unexpected ferocity. To cheer me up in that pre-Skype, pre-email era, my mother included hand-written recipes in her twice- and sometimes thrice-weekly letters, but I usually couldn't try out those recipes, because in the

Iowa of the early 1960s, supermarkets didn't carry the basic Indian ingredients.

The summer evening our first son was born in Iowa City, my father happened to be in the U.S. on a business trip, so, as soon as he heard of the birth of his first grandchild, he rushed to Iowa City for a brief, emotional reunion. And, he brought with him a surprise gift: my mother's recipe for payesh. She had selected payesh because payesh must be served at annaprasan, the ceremony marking a baby's readiness for solid food. In a society with a steep rate of infant mortality, a baby that survives long enough for the annaprasana ceremony holds the promise of family continuity. My father, a very traditional patriarch, *never* entered the kitchen at home in India. But there he was, in our rented farmhouse kitchen, carrying a small packet of basmati rice from home, lovingly stirring whole milk, scraping down the dried film of milk from the sides of the pan.

Dr. Ranu Vanikar's Royal Bengal-Maratha Payesh Recipe

As with all comfort foods, every cook improves on the handed-down recipe. My younger sister, who learned to make magic in the kitchen from watching my mother, has improvised her own version of payesh. She, too, studied in the U.S., but she went back to India and married an ethnic Maratha. She balances with ease her dual roles as a modern professional with a thriving career and a wife schooled in the art of traditional Indian homemaking. This is her recipe in her own words.

2 liters whole milk
1 can condensed milk
4 tablespoons basmati rice
1 tablespoon saffron
3 tablespoons sugar
½ cup currants
peeled and chopped pistachios and
    slivered almonds

Soak rice in water for 30 minutes. Soak saffron in ¼ cup warm milk. Boil milk in a heavy-bottomed pan. When the milk has boiled, drain water from the rice and pour the rice into the milk. Keep stirring. When the rice is half-cooked, add 3 tablespoons of sugar. Keep stirring the milk until it is reduced to half its original volume. Add 1 can of condensed milk, and keep stirring. When the consistency has thickened adequately, add saffron and the milk the saffron has been soaking in, almonds, pistachios and currants. Stir and pour into glass bowls. Serve at room temperature or chilled. Serves 6.

Instruction to impatient cooks: Remember to keep stirring while reducing the milk; this process may take a total of 1–2 hours.

BHARATI MUKHERJEE is the author of eight novels (most recently, *Miss New India, Desirable Daughters,* and *The Tree Bride*); two collections of short stories (*Darkness* and *The Middleman & Other Stories*); and the co-author, with Clark Blaise, of two books of non-fiction (*Days and Nights in Calcutta* and *The Sorrow and the Terror: The Haunting Legacy of the Air India Tragedy*), and numerous essays on immigration and American culture. She is the first naturalized U.S. citizen to win the National Book Critics' Circle Award for Best Fiction. She is an Emerita Professor of English at the University of California, Berkeley.

EDWARD KELSEY MOORE
MY BEST DIETARY INTENTIONS

I descend from a long line of home chefs who were devoted to the idea that every bite of food should be exciting and decadent. One of the great surprises of my youth was the discovery that there were people who ate meatloaf without the wrapping of latticed bacon strips I had presumed to be mandatory. Another shock was my first sighting of someone removing the brown, crisp skin from a chicken breast, an act I'd only heard about in scornful whispers. And though nearly half a century has passed since my favorite great-aunt confided the secret of her legendary yeast rolls to me, I can still picture her grin as she said, "It's all about the butter bath."

When I grew into adulthood and grew out of a healthy body mass index, I rebelled against family tradition. I adopted ways of eating and of preparing food that would have been unimaginable to my Indiana kinfolk. And that new approach to eating has probably saved my life. But the old ways die hard. The butter bath that is my gene pool keeps calling me back and my best dietary intentions have a way of going bad. In my hands, an innocent stalk of celery often becomes the delivery system for half a jar of peanut butter. I tend to make decisions about what to plant in my garden based upon how well the vegetables complement my favorite cheeses and smoked meats.

Over time, I have accepted my culinary heredity and tried to battle it a little less and celebrate it a little more. While not nearly as decadent as my kale recipe, which is really just a ham with a few kale leaves as garnish, this apple-sweet potato bar recipe is indicative of my attempt to strike a balance between what I want to eat and what I should eat. It is the distant cousin of a recipe that came to me through a kind friend who desperately wanted to save me from myself. When the recipe arrived at my door, it was spotlessly virtuous—comprised almost entirely of fiber and fruit, free from the taint of fat and sugar. Many substitutions later, however, the dessert that exited my oven bore little resemblance to its nobler relation. The applesauce of the original recipe had been swapped out for sweet potato purée. Butter replaced fat-free yogurt. Brown sugar was added because my roll baking great-aunt once told me that every apple dessert needed brown sugar. I'm happy to report that these apple-sweet potato bars still have enough fiber and fruit in them to be a little bit good for you. But I'm also glad to say that there's enough of my ancestral influence in the recipe that you'd never know it's kind of healthy.

Apple-Sweet-Potato Bars

1 cup whole wheat flour
½ cup all-purpose flour
1 teaspoon baking soda
½ teaspoon salt
1 teaspoon ground cinnamon
½ teaspoon ground cloves
⅓ cup softened butter
⅔ cup firmly packed light brown sugar
1 ¾ cups shredded (or finely chopped) peeled sweet potato
1 teaspoon vanilla extract
1 ¾ cups shredded (or finely chopped) apple (with or without peel)
1 cup raisins
¾ cup old-fashioned oats
½ cup butterscotch morsels

Microwave the shredded sweet potatoes until soft, then stir with a fork until mostly smooth. (Makes about a cup of sweet potato purée.) Stir together flours, salt, soda, cinnamon, and cloves in a bowl. In a larger bowl, cream together butter and brown sugar.* Add flour mixture to butter and sugar a third at a time, alternating with sweet potato, and stir until combined. Stir in vanilla. Stir in apple and next three ingredients.

*If you are using a standing mixer, just throw everything in together after creaming the sugar and butter and mix until thoroughly combined.

Spread batter into an 11 x 7-inch baking dish coated with cooking spray or butter.

Bake at 350 for 35–40 minutes or until a wooden toothpick inserted in the center comes out clean. Allow to cool slightly before slicing into bars.

EDWARD KELSEY MOORE is the author of the *New York Times* bestselling novel *The Supremes at Earl's All-You-Can-Eat,* published by Alfred A. Knopf in 2013. His essays and short fiction have appeared in *The New York Times* and a number of literary magazines, including *Ninth Letter, Indiana Review, African American Review,* and *Inkwell.* In addition to his writing, Edward continues to maintain a career as a professional cellist: He is the principal cellist of the New Black Music Repertory Ensemble, and also performs with a number of ensembles, including the Chicago Sinfonietta and the Joffrey Ballet Orchestra.

CURTIS SITTENFELD
HOW TO MASTER FOOD ALLERGIES*

For years and years, when people invite you over and ask if you have any dietary restrictions, you say no, then sometimes jokingly add, "Unfortunately!"

When your older daughter is a toddler and you are pregnant with your younger daughter, your husband says, "Every Friday, we should have family pizza night." You say, "Great." Four months later, you give birth to a daughter who is allergic to milk (meaning also to cheese), as well as to eggs, tree nuts, peanuts, and maybe buckwheat and flaxseed. Very early on, certain foods leave rashes around her mouth or make her vomit, so you stop giving them to her. When she is eight months old, her sister spills ice cream on her arm. Red bumps immediately rise in the places the ice cream touched.

Your daughter is officially diagnosed just before she turns one, and for her first birthday, you make her a

"cake" out of puréed sweet potatoes topped with coconut yogurt (you are now well-versed in the debate about whether coconut is a tree nut and think it's not). She feels about this cake the way most anyone would, which is that it's gross.

You scour the Internet for recommendations on how to handle multiple food allergies. You find horror stories about children dying of anaphylaxis brought on by a single bite of the wrong thing.

You read every ingredient on everything you buy at the grocery store, even when you buy more than one package of the same thing, even when you buy the same product week after week. You come to know certain products so well that when they get a new ingredient, it's like a friend getting a haircut.

You talk to a fellow "food allergy mom," the friend of a friend, who explains that your family shouldn't go out for ice cream because even if your daughter gets sorbet, the employee will use the same spoon to scoop it that he used for someone else's cone of pistachio; and your daughter shouldn't eat jelly at another family's house because that family dips their peanut buttery knives in the jelly when making sandwiches. You have always been such a good worrier, but these are things you never thought to worry about.

You stop going to restaurants as a family; you stop bringing home carryout, except occasionally and furtively, when you and your husband take turns eating it standing up in a corner of the kitchen (his preference) or sitting on the upstairs bathroom floor with the door closed (your preference).

You never give your daughter food unless you can read the ingredients of the package it came in. Otherwise, you never give her food prepared outside your kitchen.

You stop eating things in front of her that she can't eat. At all social events where there is food, which is all social events, you feel like you are her bodyguard.

You never leave the house without EpiPens.

Your husband, who barely cooked before you had children, matter-of-factly learns to make vegan doughnuts and vegan waffles and vegan whipped cream.

Because it's medically recommended that you keep exposing your older daughter to the foods your younger daughter is allergic to, you go once or twice a week with your older daughter to diners or bakeries or Vietnamese restaurants. These are delightful outings—your older daughter is excellent company and loves trying new things—at the conclusion of which you scrub your hands and hers, at the restaurant and again at home, with a vigor appropriate for performing surgery. Also, clearly, these delightful outings bum out your younger daughter.

When your daughter is two, you write an article for an online magazine pleading, while trying to seem likeable, for other parents not to let their kids litter playgrounds with snacks. The article generates thousands of comments, most of which say that you're a horrible mother and your daughter's worst problem is being your offspring. One of these posts is written by a man whose children also have food allergies.

You discover that there is a diverse, vibrant, engaged food allergy community. You fantasize about your daughter outgrowing her allergies so that you are no longer part of it.

When your daughter starts preschool, you burst into tears at the meeting with her teachers where you discuss how to handle snack time.

On Halloween, you go trick-or-treating but carry along your own bag of candy for your daughter to choose from. Your daughter takes her own cupcakes to birthday parties and her own snack on playdates.

You barely travel as a family; when you do, you pack loaves of bread and jars of sun butter in your suitcase. You FedEx soy milk to Idaho.

You go out for lunch with a kind, smart woman your age who grew up with multiple food allergies, who has injected herself several times with EpiPens, and you ask what her parents did right and wrong. You meet in a restaurant where you observe how she orders her soup and wonder if she will have a reaction during this very meal. Before you part, she says, "You're doing a good job. Your daughter will be fine." If only you could hold her to it!

You wonder if it's all because you ate too many peanut M&M's when you were pregnant. At the same time, you decide that if you had it to do over again, the minute your daughter emerged from the birth canal, you'd have chewed up a peanut and spit it from your mouth into hers.

Other things you'd have done to prevent her allergies, if only time-travel were possible and if only you'd known: gotten a dog; renounced your dishwasher; become Amish.

You lie awake at night fretting about when your daughter is old enough for sleepovers, or for kissing, or for college. Also, can she ever go camping?

You play a game in your head that, if it had a name, would be called What Would You Do to Make Her Allergies Go Away?

Give up your career as a writer: Yes.
Let your left hand be cut off: Yes.
Let your right hand be cut off: Yes, but only instead of rather than in addition to the left hand.

→

Cut off your right hand yourself using a chef's knife: Yes.
Gain 20 pounds: Yes.
Gain 100 pounds: Somewhat surprisingly, no.

When another pre-school mom tells you her son said he feels "sad" for your daughter because she's "sick," you understand that the mom is proud of her son's sensitivity; nevertheless, you detest this woman.

Those parents who complain about not being able to send their kids to school with the PB&J they love? Those airplane passengers who groan audibly when the flight attendant announces they won't be serving peanuts today? Those codgers who say allergies didn't exist when they were young and it's just a bunch of helicopter-parenting? You detest them, too.

But you feel enormous gratitude towards the parents who write "sun butter" on the plastic bags they send sandwiches to school in, or who go over the exact menu for their kid's birthday party and show no irritation when they say, "Bagged carrots," and you ask, "Bagged carrots that you'll buy bagged or bag yourself?"

You start going as a family to an ice cream parlor where your older daughter and your husband get ice cream and you and your younger daughter bring coconut bars from home. You frantically wipe down the table and chairs before you sit. You know this excursion would probably seem depressing from the outside; secretly, from the inside, you consider it slightly depressing. But mostly you consider it festive and triumphant. Now your daughter knows what an ice cream parlor looks like!

You understand that into every life a little rain must fall but just wish the rain had fallen on you. Obviously, to some extent, it is falling on you. But you wish it had fallen on you completely.

As much trouble as her allergies are, you never wish your daughter was anyone other than her hilarious, stubborn, singing, dancing, mermaid-obsessed, food allergic self.

*You cannot, it turns out, master food allergies. But you actually can make cookies that are both safe for your daughter and delicious.

Nut-free, Egg-free, Milk-free Sun Butter Cookies

(Adapted from the peanut butter cookie recipe in *Peas and Thank You* by Sarah Matheny)

½ cup Earth Balance Organic Whipped Buttery Spread
¾ cup sun butter
½ cup brown sugar
¾ cup powdered sugar
½ teaspoon vanilla extract
1 teaspoon baking powder
½ teaspoon baking soda
¾ teaspoon salt
1 cup whole wheat pastry flour
½ cup all-purpose flour
½ cup Enjoy Life brand Semi-Sweet Chocolate Mini-Chips

Preheat oven to 350. Blend baking powder, baking soda, salt, and flour. Set aside.

With a stand mixer, blend buttery spread, sun butter, sugars, and vanilla. Gradually pour the dry mixture into the wet mixture and combine.

Add chocolate chips.

Set dough in refrigerator for 30 minutes. Remove, and use a tablespoon to create a dozen dough balls.

Bake for 10–12 minutes.

CURTIS SITTENFELD is the bestselling author of five novels: *Prep, The Man of My Dreams, American Wife, Sisterland,* and *Eligible.* Her books have been selected by *The New York Times, Time, Entertainment Weekly,* and *People* for their "Ten Best Books of the Year" lists, optioned for television and film, and translated into 25 languages. Her non-fiction has appeared in *The New York Times, Time, Vanity Fair, The Atlantic, Slate,* and "This American Life." She lives with her family in St. Louis, Missouri.

TIM KREIDER
RECIPE FOR HEARTBREAK

Kati Jo's Heartbreak Pie Crust
(makes one 9-inch crust)

1 cup flour
½ teaspoon salt
1 tablespoon butter
⅓ cup vegetable shortening
1 medium heartbreak (approx. 6
   months)
ice water (approx. ½ cup)
preparation time: approx. 15 years

Place all ingredients and rolling pin in freezer at least 30 minutes before beginning.

Meet Kati Jo in college; should be beautiful, blond, with a lyrical prose style. Make sure she is unavailable, preferably with much handsomer boyfriend. Store image of her in diaphanous midriff-baring dress for later use. Preheat to 425.

Sift together flour and salt.

When Kati Jo publishes first novel, combine unrequited lust with professional envy to form unattainable ideal of all that you desire.

Using fingers, knives, or biscuit cutter, cut butter and shortening into flour

mixture until fats are broken up into nodules the size of Champagne grapes, handling dough as little as possible.

Correspond w/ Kati Jo re. writing, books, relationships, etc., for approx. 1 decade. Reduce heat; simmer through 2 marriages.

Mix ice water into flour mixture, spoonful by spoonful, until dough can form a ball. This is a crucial phase— too little water and dough will crack; too much and it will stick.

As soon as Kati Jo's second marriage ends, commence long-distance affair (min. 1,000 miles). Increase heat to high until ingredients break down. Should take no more than 4 visits (phoning frequently throughout). Total duration: 3–4 months.

Roll out crust onto clean, floured countertop, not pressing but rolling in firm, even strokes from center outward, using ice water to mend any cracks.

Crouch, weeping, on bare, filthy surface, like bathroom floor, for roughly same amount of time as affair.

Pour in filling, lay on lattice top crust if desired, crimp edges, then brush top with milk and sprinkle with sugar. Extra dough can be sprinkled with sugar and cinnamon, rolled up and baked to make a treat called "Roly-Polys" that children love.

After 1 year, exchange bittersweet e-mails until Kati Jo enters third marriage.

Enjoy.

TIM KREIDER is a frequent contributor to *The New York Times* and *The New Yorker*. His cartoon *The Pain—When Will It End?* has become a cult favorite and has been collected in three books. He is the author of *We Learn Nothing*, a collection of essays and cartoons published by Simon and Schuster. He lives in New York and an Undisclosed Location on the Chesapeake Bay.

JULIA ALVAREZ
MOM'S BAD GINGER COOKIES

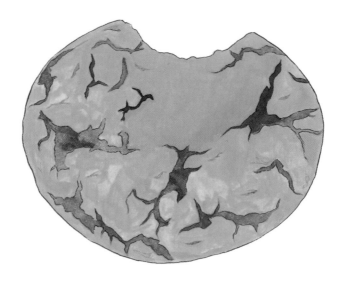

From the time she first met me until she died 13 years ago, my husband's mother tried to get me to eat desserts. She'd set down a fresh rhubarb pie at the Sunday supper table or remove the cake cover from her apple-walnut cake, and look hopefully in my direction. I don't think it was just that she couldn't accept that I didn't want a serving. She couldn't understand my excuse. "I don't eat desserts," I kept saying. "They're too sweet."

"But desserts are *supposed* to be sweet," she'd counter.

"I know," I'd say. "That's why I don't eat them."

Of course, I felt bad. I had married into a Nebraska farm family where being a good cook and having an appreciative appetite were requirements for acceptance. I wondered if I'd ever fit in.

About a year before she died, Mom came to Sunday supper at our house close to tears. She had been trying out a recipe for ginger cookies, and she had gotten interrupted by Dad in the middle of mixing the ingredients. She must have shorted the molasses because the ginger cookies were very gingery but not all that sweet.

My husband dismissed her protests. Mom always preceded a serving of one of her delicious recipes by predicting some flaw in the results. But when dessert time came, Bill bit into a ginger cookie, and his honest face could not disguise the truth. "You're right, Mom. They could use a little more molasses."

Mom's eyes welled up. She had become increasingly fragile, and these once-a-week desserts were her contribution to our family gatherings. For the hundredth time in our marriage I wondered what Nebraska Lutherans have against little white lies?

I reached for one of those bad ginger cookies, prepared to lie to make Mom feel better. Just the shock of seeing me eat dessert stopped Mom's tears. I took a bite, and then a second bite. "Mom, they're really good!" I was not lying. These cookies resembled English tea biscuits, just the amount of sweetness I like.

From then on, Mom kept me supplied. Before I went on book tours, she'd cook up a batch of ginger cookies for me to take on the road. I kept promising myself to go over to her condo and learn to make them. But somehow I was always too busy.

After Mom's death, we found a box of ginger cookies in her freezer. I parceled them out, having one a week to make them last. Each time I took a bite and that spicy tingling filled my mouth, I thought of how—along with all other losses that came with losing Mom—I would soon be losing the taste of her ginger cookies. As we cleaned out her condo, I searched her kitchen drawers and recipe box, but I could not find her ginger cookie recipe.

Since then, my husband and I have been trying to come up with a recipe. Each time we taste our latest version, we sadly shake our heads. Not quite as good as Mom's bad ginger cookies. But we're almost there.

Mom's Bad Ginger Cookies

1 stick butter, melted
1 cup Grandma's molasses, light (Bill and I disagree on this one. I say less than a cup, he says a cup.)
3 cups flour (Bill says, 1 cup, coarse whole-wheat flour; 2 cups, white flour. I say, more whole wheat and less white.)

3 teaspoons ginger powder
1 teaspoon soda
chopped crystallized ginger (optional)
brown sugar for topping (optional)

Mix together and roll out ¼ to ½-inch thick on floured board.

Cut out and put on oiled baking sheet.

Bill says for a treat, sweet-tooth cooks could try mixing in some chopped-up crystallized ginger. He also suggests sprinkling a little brown sugar on top of cookies right before baking. I say leave well enough alone.

Bake 8–10 minutes or until done in 350-degree oven.

JULIA ALVAREZ has written novels (*How the García Girls Lost Their Accents, In the Time of the Butterflies, ¡Yo!, In the Name of Salomé, Saving the World*), collections of poems (*Homecoming, The Other Side/ El Otro Lado, The Woman I Kept to Myself*), nonfiction (*Something to Declare, Once Upon A Quinceañera, A Wedding in Haiti*), and numerous books for young readers (including the *Tía Lola Stories series, Before We Were Free, finding miracles,* and *Return to Sender*) and, most recently, *Where Do They Go?* A recipient of a 2013 National Medal of Arts, Alvarez is currently a writer in residence at Middlebury College.

NATALIE EVE GARRETT
DISGUSTINGLY GOOD COOKIES

A few years ago, I came across an unusual cookie recipe that called for chickpeas instead of flour. I thought it was potentially gross and too health-foody, but I loved the warning at the end, something along the lines of: *do not try the dough, it is disgusting.*

Laughing, I told my husband: "There's this cookie recipe that claims that the cookies are good, but the *dough* is disgusting. Whaaaat?!" He smiled, probably amused more by me and my obsessive recipe hunting and gathering than anything else. Anyhow, I didn't make them.

But I thought about them. The recipe got stuck in my head the way some people get songs stuck in their head.

Although my daughter says songs don't get really stuck in your head, they get stuck "in your mouth," and maybe it's the same with recipes? I wanted a taste. I wondered what the texture and smell were like, what dark magic transformed chickpeas into dough. After all, I like chickpeas well enough, and I've always enjoyed sweet red bean desserts. And of course chocolate comes from beans, too. Maybe the dough wasn't even disgusting. Maybe, instead, it was disgustingly *good*.

Six months later, I finally made chickpea cookies, and they changed my life forever. I fixated on them, started writing and publishing my own recipes, and, in an oblique way, they even led me to create this book.

Since then, I've made gobs of these cookies—I'm probably at least 30% chickpea by now—and the taste is strangely addictive, as is the process of making something so mysterious. Over time, I've adjusted the recipe while also improvising and honing recipes for other chickpea creations: spicy chickpea brownies, chickpea peanut butter bars with raspberry jam, pumpkin-chickpea-almond-butter bars, roasted maple-coconut chickpeas, sour cream blueberry chickpea muffins. For special occasions, I make a divine mint chocolate chickpea cake. My kids even associate sweets with chickpeas, which sometimes makes me feel like I'm "winning" at parenting.

This is my recipe for chickpea cookies, originally published in The Hairpin, inspired by Texanerin, and now new and improved. They have a soft, chewy texture, a nutty, lightly sweet flavor, and lots of dark chocolate chips. I dare you to give them a try. And, while you're at it, please feel free to sample the dough.

Natalie's Chickpea Chocolate Chip Banana Cookies

1 ½ cups chickpeas

heaping ½ cup peanut butter (or other nut or seed butter)

¼ cup honey

2 teaspoons vanilla

½ banana

1 teaspoon baking powder

heaping ½ cup dark chocolate chips

¼ teaspoon sea salt

extra sea salt for sprinkling on top

Preheat the oven to 350, then line a cookie sheet with parchment paper.

Measure out your chickpeas. If you're using canned chickpeas, dry them on paper towels first and peel them if you've got the time. (The dough will be slightly smoother if you do, but they'll be great either way.)

Purée the chickpeas in a food processor fitted with a steel blade. Scrape down the edges, and blend for several minutes until the dough is smooth.

Add all of the remaining ingredients except the dark chocolate chips and extra sea salt and pulse until combined.

Add the chocolate chips and mix. The dough will be quite sticky now.

Spoon the dough onto parchment paper, making approximately 16 cookies. Flatten each cookie very slightly with a fork and sprinkle sea salt to taste.

Bake for 11–13 minutes, and let me know what you think.

NATALIE EVE GARRETT is an artist, writer, and the editor of *The Artists' and Writers' Cookbook.* She is interested in making things that convey a sense of humor and magic, with a disarming twist. Her work can often be seen on The Hairpin. A graduate of Yale University and the University of Pennsylvania's School of Design, Natalie lives in a town just outside DC and along the Potomac River with her husband and two children. More information can be found at natalieevegarrett.com.

ACKNOWLEDGEMENTS

This book was a labor of love, and it would not have been possible without the generosity of so many people: my agent, Jody Kahn, who believed in the book in the very beginning, back when it sounded crazy, stayed with it over time as it got even crazier, and offered her expertise and friendship along the way; my wonderful publisher Craig Cohen, designer Krzysztof Poluchowicz, and editor Will Luckman; illustrator and best pal Amy Jean Porter, who created gorgeous works of art and helped plot our forthcoming tropical island cookbook show; "bioluminescent girl" Edith Zimmerman, a true friend and my inspiration every time; and pen pal Jessica Grose for a zillion sassy-slash-wise emails. Thanks to all my dear ones—you know who you are. And thank you to my family for offering clarity, support, and hugs always. Finally, I'm forever grateful for the artists and writers who shared their stories and recipes with me. It's been an honor and a thrill to work with each of you. Many thanks.

PERMISSIONS

The Artists' and Writers' Cookbook:
A Collection of Stories with Recipes

Introduction, compilation & editing © 2016 by Natalie Eve Garrett
Illustrations and hand lettering © 2016 Amy Jean Porter
Illustrations were created in gouache and ink on paper.

Published in the United States by powerHouse Books,
a division of powerHouse Cultural Entertainment, Inc.
37 Main Street, Brooklyn, NY 11201-1021
telephone 212.604.9074, fax 212.366.5247
e-mail: info@powerHouseBooks.com
website: www.powerHouseBooks.com

First edition, 2016

Library of Congress Control Number: 2016943854

Hardcover ISBN 978-1-57687-788-3

Printing and binding by Midas Printing, Inc., China

Book design by Krzysztof Poluchowicz
Cover design by Amy Jean Porter
Art direction by Natalie Eve Garrett

10 9 8 7 6 5 4 3 2

Printed and bound in China

ANTHONY DOERR   LEANNE SHAPTON   MAILE MELOY

RACHEL FEINSTEIN   ED RUSCHA   NEIL GAIMAN

GREGORY CREWDSON   EDWIDGE DANTICAT   ALICE

JOY GARNETT   APRIL GORNIK   KATE

JAMES FRANCO   AMBER DERMONT   JAMES SIENA

FRANCESCA LIA BLOCK   NELSON DEMILLE   ANN HOOD

LAUREL NAKADATE   RICK MOODY   JEFFERY RENARD ALLEN

KAMROOZ ARAM   NIKKI GIOVANNI   RUTH OZEK

PETER HO DAVIES   ANN CRAVEN   LEV GROSSMAN

ANA CASTILLO   PATRICIA MARX   SHARON OLDS

SANFORD BIGGERS   LIZA LOU   ED PARK   DANIYAL

AÏDA RUILOVA   MANIL SURI   JESSICA STOLLER

EDWARD KELSEY MOORE   CURTIS SITTENFELD   TIM